In *Our Man in Havana,* the greatest of living English novelists spins the absorbing and ironic tale of one Mr. Wormold. No lover of heroics, he is nonetheless drawn into the cloak-and-dagger world of high-paying, high-level espionage. From a comfortable position on the fringe of that world, he plies an elaborate scheme of make-believe, inventing agents, manufacturing intelligence reports, and milking the expense account for all it's worth.

Neither sinister nor evil in intent, he creates a fiction more dangerous than any reality—a military secret, a manhunt, and more than one very real murder.

"A uniquely satisfying brew."   —*Newsweek*

"Ross MacDonald, John Le Carré and any number of other suspense novelists learned how it ought to be done from Graham Greene, but very few have approached his massively professional talent for world-weary disenchantment combined with smooth showmanship."   —*Boston Globe*

OUR MAN IN HAVANA
was originally published in the U.S.A. by The Viking Press, Inc.

Books by Graham Greene

*Published by POCKET BOOKS

Graham Greene

OUR MAN
IN
HAVANA

PUBLISHED BY POCKET BOOKS NEW YORK

OUR MAN IN HAVANA

Heinemann Bodley Head edition published 1958
POCKET BOOK edition published December, 1974

Standard Book Number: 671-78466-8.
This POCKET BOOK edition is published by arrangement
with The Viking Press, Inc. Copyright, ©, 1958, by William Heinemann, Ltd. All rights reserved. This book, or
portions thereof, may not be reproduced by any means
without permission of the publisher: The Viking Press, Inc.,
625 Madison Ave., New York, N.Y. 10022.
Front cover illustration by Alan Magee.
Printed in the U.S.A.

And the sad man is cock of all his jests.

—George Herbert

PART I

[1]

i

"That nigger going down the street," said Dr. Hasselbacher standing in the Wonder Bar, "he reminds me of you, Mr. Wormold." It was typical of Dr. Hasselbacher that after fifteen years of friendship he still used the prefix Mr.—friendship proceeded with the slowness and assurance of a careful diagnosis. On Wormold's death-bed, when Dr. Hasselbacher came to feel his failing pulse, he would perhaps become Jim.

The negro was blind in one eye and one leg was shorter than the other; he wore an ancient felt hat and his ribs showed through his torn shirt like a ship's under demolition. He walked at the edge of the pavement, beyond the yellow and pink pillars of a colonnade, in the hot January sun, and he counted every step as he went. As he passed the Wonder Bar, going up Virdudes, he had reached "1,369." He had to move slowly to give time for so long a numeral. "One thousand three hundred and seventy." He was a familiar figure near the National Square, where he would sometimes linger and stop his counting long enough to sell a packet of pornographic photographs to a tourist. Then he would take up his count where he had left it. At the end of the day, like an energetic passenger on a trans-Atlantic liner, he must have known to a yard how far he had walked.

"Joe?" Wormold asked. "I don't see any resemblance. Except the limp, of course," but instinctively he took a quick look at himself in the mirror marked Cerveza Tropical, as though he might really have been so broken down and darkened during his walk from the store in the old town. But the face which looked back at him was only a little discoloured by the dust from the harbour-works; it was still the same, anxious and criss-crossed and fortyish: much younger than Dr. Hasselbacher's, yet a stranger

might have felt certain it would be extinguished sooner—
the shadow was there already, the anxieties which are
beyond the reach of a tranquilliser. The negro limped out
of sight, round the corner of the Paseo. The day was full
of bootblacks.

"I didn't mean the limp. You don't see the likeness?"

"No."

"He's got two ideas in his head," Dr. Hasselbacher
explained, "to do his job and to keep count. And, of
course, he's British."

"I still don't see . . ." Wormold cooled his mouth with
his morning daiquiri. Seven minutes to get to the Wonder
Bar: seven minutes back to the store: six minutes for
companionship. He looked at his watch. He remembered
that it was one minute slow.

"He's reliable, you can depend on him, that's all I
meant," said Dr. Hasselbacher with impatience. "How's
Milly?"

"Wonderful," Wormold said. It was his invariable answer, but he meant it.

"Seventeen on the seventeenth, eh?"

"That's right." He looked quickly over his shoulder as
though somebody were hunting him and then at his watch
again. "You'll be coming to split a bottle with us?"

"I've never failed yet, Mr. Wormold. Who else will be
there?"

"Well, I thought just the three of us. You see, Cooper's
gone home, and poor Marlowe's in hospital still, and Milly
doesn't seem to care for any of this new crowd at the
Consulate. So I thought we'd keep it quiet, in the
family."

"I'm honoured to be one of the family, Mr. Wormold."

"Perhaps a table at the Nacional—or would you say
that wasn't quite—well, suitable?"

"This isn't England or Germany, Mr. Wormold. Girls
grow up quickly in the tropics."

A shutter across the way creaked open and then regularly blew to in the slight breeze from the sea, click clack
like an ancient clock. Wormold said, "I must be off."

"Phastkleaners will get on without you, Mr. Wormold."
It was a day of uncomfortable truths. "Like my patients,"
Dr. Hasselbacher added with kindliness.

"People have to get ill, they don't have to buy vacuum cleaners."

"But you charge them more."

"And get only twenty per cent for myself. One can't save much on twenty per cent."

"This is not an age for saving, Mr. Wormold."

"I must—for Milly. If something happened to me . . ."

"We none of us have a great expectation of life nowadays, so why worry?"

"All these disturbances are very bad for trade. What's the good of a vacuum cleaner if the power's cut off?"

"I could manage a small loan, Mr. Wormold."

"No, no. It's not like that. My worry isn't this year's or even next year's, it's a long-term worry."

"Then it's not worth calling a worry. We live in an atomic age, Mr. Wormold. Push a button—piff bang—where are we? Another Scotch, please."

"And that's another thing. You know what the firm has done now? They've sent me an Atomic Pile Cleaner."

"Really? I didn't know science had got that far."

"Oh, of course, there's nothing atomic about it—it's only a name. Last year there was the Turbo Jet; this year it's the Atomic. It works off the light-plug just the same as the other."

"Then why worry?" Dr. Hasselbacher repeated like a theme tune, leaning into his whisky.

"They don't realise that sort of name may go down in the States, but not here, where the clergy are preaching all the time against the misuse of science. Milly and I went to the Cathedral last Sunday—you know how she is about Mass, thinks she'll convert me, I wouldn't wonder. Well, Father Mendez spent half an hour describing the effect of a hydrogen bomb. Those who believe in heaven on earth, he said, are creating a hell—he made it sound that way too—it was very lucid. How do you think I liked it on Monday morning when I had to make a window display of the new Atomic Pile Suction Cleaner? It wouldn't have surprised me if one of the wild boys around here had broken the window. Catholic Action, Christ the King, all that stuff. I don't know what to do about it, Hasselbacher."

"Sell one to Father Mendez for the Bishop's palace."

"But he's satisfied with the Turbo. It was a good machine. Of course this one is too. Improved suction for bookcases. You know I wouldn't sell anyone a machine that wasn't good."

"I know, Mr. Wormold. Can't you just change the name?"

"They won't let me. They are proud of it. They think it's the best phrase anyone has thought up since 'It beats as it sweeps as it cleans.' You know they had something called an air-purifying pad with the Turbo. Nobody minded—it was a good gadget, but yesterday a woman came in and looked at the Atomic Pile and she asked whether a pad that size could really absorb all the radio-activity. And what about Strontium 90? she asked."

"I could give you a medical certificate," said Dr. Hasselbacher.

"Do you never worry about anything?"

"I have a secret defence, Mr. Wormold. I am interested in life."

"So am I, but . . ."

"You are interested in a person, not in life, and people die or leave us—I'm sorry; I wasn't referring to your wife. But if you are interested in life it never lets you down. I am interested in the blueness of the cheese. You don't do crosswords, do you, Mr. Wormold? I do, and they are like people: one reaches an end. I can finish any crossword within an hour, but I have a discovery concerned with the blueness of cheese that will never come to a conclusion—although of course one dreams that perhaps a time might come . . . One day I must show you my laboratory."

"I must be going, Hasselbacher."

"You should dream more, Mr. Wormold. Reality in our century is not something to be faced."

ii

When Wormold arrived at his store in Lamparilla Street, Milly had not yet returned from her American convent school, and in spite of the two figures he could see through the door, the shop seemed to him empty. How empty! And so it would remain until Milly came back. He was aware whenever he entered the shop of a vacuum that had nothing to do with his cleaners. No customer could fill it, particularly not the one who stood there now looking too spruce for Havana and reading a leaflet in English on the Atomic Pile, pointedly neglecting Wormold's assistant. Lopez was an impatient man who did not like to waste his time away from the Spanish edition of *Confidential*. He was glaring at the stranger and making no attempt to win him over.

"*Buenos días*," Wormold said. He looked at all strangers in the shop with an habitual suspicion. Ten years ago a man had entered the shop, posing as a customer, and he had guilelessly sold him a sheep's wool for the high-gloss finishing on his car. He had been a plausible impostor, but no one could be a less likely purchaser of a vacuum cleaner than this man. Tall and elegant, in his stone-coloured tropical suit, and wearing an exclusive tie, he carried with him the breath of beaches and the leathery smell of a good club: you expected him to say, "The Ambassador will see you in a minute." His cleaning would always be arranged for him—by an ocean or a valet.

"Don't speak the lingo, I'm afraid," the stranger answered. The slang word was a blemish on his suit, like an egg-stain after breakfast. "You are British, aren't you?"

"Yes."

"I mean—really British. British passport and all that."

"Yes. Why?"

"One likes to do business with a British firm. One knows where one is, if you see what I mean."

"What can I do for you?"

"Well, first, I just wanted to look around." He spoke as though he were in a bookshop. "I couldn't make your chap understand that."

"You are looking for a vacuum cleaner?"

"Well, not exactly looking."

"I mean, you are thinking of buying one?"

"That's it, old man, you've hit it on the nail." Wormold had the impression that the man had chosen his tone because he felt it matched the store—a protective colouring in Lamparilla Street; the breeziness certainly didn't match his clothes. One can't successfully follow St. Paul's technique of being all things to all men without a change of suit.

Wormold said briskly, "You couldn't do better than the Atomic Pile."

"I notice one here called the Turbo."

"That too is a very good cleaner. Have you a big apartment?"

"Well, not exactly big."

"Here, you see, you get two sets of brushes—this one for waxing and this for polishing—oh no, I think it's the other way round. The Turbo is air-powered."

"What does that mean?"

"Well, of course, it's . . . well, it's what it says, air-powered."

"This funny little bit here—what's that for?"

"That's a two-way carpet nozzle."

"You don't say so? Isn't that interesting? Why two-way?"

"You push and you pull."

"The things they think up," the stranger said. "I suppose you sell a lot of these?"

"I'm the only agent here."

"All the important people, I suppose, have to have an Atomic Pile?"

"Or a Turbo Jet."

"Government offices?"

"Of course. Why?"

"What's good enough for a government office should be good enough for me."

"You might prefer our Midget Make-Easy."

"Make what easy?"

"The full title is Midget Make-Easy Air-Powered Suction Small Home Cleaner."

"That word air-powered again."

"I'm not responsible for it."

"Don't get riled, old man."

"Personally I hate the words Atomic Pile," Wormold said with sudden passion. He was deeply disturbed. It occurred to him that this stranger might be an inspector sent from the head office in London or New York. In that case they should hear nothing but the truth.

"I see what you mean. It's not a happy choice. Tell me, do you service these things?"

"Quarterly. Free of charge during the period of guarantee."

"I meant yourself."

"I send Lopez."

"The sullen chap?"

"I'm not much of a mechanic. When I touch one of these things it somehow seems to give up working."

"Don't you drive a car?"

"Yes, but if there's anything wrong, my daughter sees to it."

"Oh yes, your daughter. Where's she?"

"At school. Now let me show you this snap-action coupling," but of course, when he tried to demonstrate, it wouldn't couple. He pushed and screwed. "Faulty part," he said desperately.

"Let me try," the stranger said, and in the coupling went as smooth as you could wish.

"How old is your daughter?"

"Sixteen," he said and was angry with himself for answering.

"Well," the stranger said, "I must be getting along. Enjoyed our chat."

"Wouldn't you like to watch a cleaner at work? Lopez here would give you a demonstration."

"Not at the moment. I'll be seeing you again—here or there," the man said with a vague and insolent confidence and was gone out of the door before Wormold thought to give him a trade-card. In the square at the top of Lamparilla Street he was swallowed up among the pimps and lottery sellers of the Havana noon.

Lopez said, "He never intended to buy."

"What did he want then?"

"Who knows? He looked a long time through the window at me. I think perhaps if you had not come in, he would have asked me to find him a girl."

"A girl?"

He thought of the day ten years ago and then with uneasiness of Milly, and he wished he had not answered so many questions. He also wished that the snap-action coupling had coupled for once with a snap.

[2]

He could distinguish the approach of Milly like that of a police-car from a long way off. Whistles instead of sirens warned him of her coming. She was accustomed to walk from the bus stop in the Avenida de Belgica, but today the wolves seemed to be operating from the direction of Compostella. They were not dangerous wolves, he had reluctantly to admit that. The salute which had begun about her thirteenth birthday was really one of respect, for even by the high Havana standard Milly was beautiful. She had hair the colour of pale honey, dark eyebrows, and her pony-trim was shaped by the best barber in town. She paid no open attention to the whistles, they only made her step the higher—seeing her walk, you could almost believe in levitation. Silence would have seemed like an insult to her now.

Unlike Wormold, who believed in nothing, Milly was a Catholic: he had been made to promise her mother that before they married. Now her mother, he supposed, was of no faith at all, but she had left a Catholic on his hands. It brought Milly closer to Cuba than he could come

himself. He believed that in the rich families the custom
of keeping a duenna lingered still, and sometimes it
seemed to him that Milly too carried a duenna about with
her, invisible to all eyes but her own. In church, where
she looked more lovely than in any other place, wearing
her feather-weight mantilla embroidered with leaves
transparent as winter, the duenna was always seated by
her side, to observe that her back was straight, her face
covered at the suitable moment, the sign of the cross
correctly performed. Small boys might suck sweets with
impunity around her or giggle from behind the pillars, she
sat with the rigidity of a nun, following the Mass in a
small gilt-edged missal bound in a morocco the colour of
her hair (she had chosen it herself). The same invisible
duenna saw to it that she ate fish on Friday, fasted on
Ember Days and attended Mass not only on Sundays and
the special feasts of the church, but also on her saint's
day. Milly was her home-name: her given name was
Seraphina—in Cuba "a double of the second class," a
mysterious phrase which reminded Wormold of the race-
track.

It had been long before Wormold realised that the
duenna was not always by her side. Milly was meticulous
in her behaviour at meals and had never neglected her
night-prayers, as he had good reason to know since, even
as a child, she had kept him waiting, to mark him out as
the non-Catholic he was, before her bedroom door until
she had finished. A light burnt continually in front of the
image of Our Lady of Guadalupe. He remembered how he
had overheard her at the age of four praying, "Hail
Mary, quite contrary."

One day however, when Milly was thirteen, he had
been summoned to the convent school of the American
Sisters of Clare in the white rich suburb of Vedado. There
he learnt for the first time how the duenna left Milly
under the religious plaque by the grilled gateway of the
school. The complaint was of a serious nature: she had
set fire to a small boy called Thomas Earl Parkman,
Junior. It was true, the Reverend Mother admitted, that
Earl, as he was known in the school, had pulled Milly's

hair first, but this she considered in no way justified Milly's action which might well have had serious results if another girl had not pushed Earl into a fountain. Milly's only defence of her conduct had been that Earl was a Protestant and if there was going to be a persecution Catholics could always beat Protestants at that game.

"But how did she set Earl on fire?"

"She put petrol on the tail of his shirt."

"Petrol!"

"Lighter-fluid, and then she struck a match. We think she must have been smoking in secret."

"It's a most extraordinary story."

"I guess you don't know Milly then. I must tell you, Mr. Wormold, our patience has been sadly strained."

Apparently, six months before setting fire to Earl, Milly had circulated round her art-class a set of postcards of the world's great pictures.

"I don't see what's wrong in that."

"At the age of twelve, Mr. Wormold, a child shouldn't confine her appreciation to the nude, however classical the paintings."

"They were all nude?"

"All except Goya's Draped Maja. But she had her in the nude version too."

Wormold had been forced to fling himself on Reverend Mother's mercy—he was a poor non-believing father with a Catholic child, the American convent was the only Catholic school in Havana which was not Spanish, and he couldn't afford a governess. They wouldn't want him to send her to the Hiram C. Truman School, would they? And it would be breaking the promise he had made to his wife. He wondered in private whether it was his duty to find a new wife, but the nuns might not put up with that and in any case he still loved Milly's mother.

Of course he spoke to Milly and her explanation had the virtue of simplicity.

"Why did you set fire to Earl?"

"I was tempted by the devil," she said.

"Milly, please be sensible."

"Saints have been tempted by the devil."

"You are not a saint."

"Exactly. That's why I fell." The chapter was closed—at any rate it would be closed that afternoon between four and six in the confessional. Her duenna was back at her side and would see to that. If only, he thought, I could know for certain when the duenna takes her day off.

There had been also the question of smoking in secret.

"Are you smoking cigarettes?" he asked her.

"No."

Something in her manner made him re-phrase the question. "Have you ever smoked at all, Milly?"

"Only cheroots," she said.

Now that he heard the whistles warning him of her approach he wondered why Milly was coming up Lamparilla from the direction of the harbour instead of from the Avenida de Belgica. But when he saw her he saw the reason too. She was followed by a young shop assistant who carried a parcel so large that it obscured his face. Wormold realised sadly that she had been shopping again. He went upstairs to their apartment above the store and presently he could hear her superintending in another room the disposal of her purchases. There was a thump, a rattle and a clang of metal. "Put it there," she said, and, "No, there." Drawers opened and closed. She began to drive nails into the wall. A piece of plaster on his side shot out and fell into the salad; the daily maid had laid a cold lunch.

Milly came in strictly on time. It was always hard for him to disguise his sense of her beauty, but the invisible duenna looked coldly through him as though he were an undesirable suitor. It had been a long time now since the duenna had taken a holiday; he almost regretted her assiduity, and sometimes he would have been glad to see Earl burn again. Milly said grace and crossed herself and he sat respectfully with his head lowered until she had finished. It was one of her longer graces, which probably meant that she was not very hungry, or that she was stalling for time.

"Had a good day, Father?" she asked politely. It was

the kind of remark a wife might have made after many years.

"Not so bad, and you?" He became a coward when he watched her; he hated to oppose her in anything, and he tried to avoid for so long as possible the subject of her purchases. He knew that her monthly allowance had gone two weeks ago on some ear-rings she had fancied and a small statue of St. Seraphina.

"I got tops marks today in Dogma and Morals."

"Fine, fine. What were the questions?"

"I did best on Venial Sin."

"I saw Dr. Hasselbacher this morning," he said with apparent irrelevance.

She replied politely, "I hope he was well." The duenna, he considered, was overdoing it. People praised Catholic schools for teaching deportment, but surely deportment was intended only to impress strangers. He thought sadly, But I *am* a stranger. He was unable to follow her into her strange world of candles and lace and holy water and genuflections. Sometimes he felt that he had no child.

"He's coming in for a drink on your birthday. I thought we might go afterwards to a night-club."

"A night-club!" The duenna must have momentarily looked elsewhere as Milly exclaimed, "O Gloria Patri."

"You always used to say Alleluia."

"That was in Lower Four. Which night-club?"

"I thought perhaps the Nacional."

"Not the Shanghai Theatre?"

"Certainly not the Shanghai Theatre. I can't think how you've even heard of the place."

"In a school things get around."

Wormold said, "We haven't discussed your present. A seventeenth birthday is no ordinary one. I was wondering . . ."

"Really and truly," Milly said, "there's nothing in the world I want."

Wormold remembered with apprehension that enormous package. If she had really gone out and got everything she wanted . . . He pleaded with her, "Surely there must be something you still want."

"Nothing. Really nothing."

"A new swim-suit," he suggested desperately.

"Well, there is one thing . . . But I thought we might count it as a Christmas present too, and next year's and the year after that . . ."

"Good heavens, what is it?"

"You wouldn't have to worry about presents any more for a long time."

"Don't tell me you want a Jaguar."

"Oh no, this is quite a small present. Not a car. This would last for years. It's an awfully economical idea. It might even, in a way, save petrol."

"Save petrol?"

"And today I got all the etceteras—with my own money."

"You haven't got any money. I had to lend you three pesos for Saint Seraphina."

"But my credit's good."

"Milly, I've told you over and over again I won't have you buying on credit. Anyway it's my credit, not yours, and my credit's going down all the time."

"Poor Father. Are we on the edge of ruin?"

"Oh, I expect things will pick up again when the disturbances are over."

"I thought there were always disturbances in Cuba. If the worst came to the worst I could go out and work, couldn't I?"

"What at?"

"Like Jane Eyre I could be a governess."

"Who would take you?"

"Señor Perez."

"Milly, what on earth are you talking about? He's living with his fourth wife, you're a Catholic . . ."

"I might have a special vocation to sinners," Milly said.

"Milly, what nonsense you talk. Anyway, I'm not ruined. Not yet. As far as I know. Milly, what have you been buying?"

"Come and see." He followed her into her bedroom. A saddle lay on her bed; a bridle and bit were hanging on the wall from the nails she had driven in (she had knocked off a heel from her best evening shoes in doing it); reins were draped between the light brackets; a whip was propped up on the dressing-table. He said hopelessly, "Where's the horse?" and half expected it to appear from the bathroom.

"In a stable near the Country Club. Guess what she's called."

"How can I?"

"Seraphina. Isn't it just like the hand of God?"

"But, Milly, I can't possibly afford . . ."

"You needn't pay for her all at once. She's a chestnut."

"What difference does the colour make?"

"She's in the stud-book. Out of Santa Teresa by Ferdinand of Castile. She would have cost twice as much, but she fouled a fetlock jumping wire. There's nothing wrong, only a kind of lump, so they can't show her."

"I don't mind if it's a quarter the price. Business is too bad, Milly."

"But I've explained to you, you needn't pay all at once. You can pay over the years."

"And I'll still be paying for it when it's dead."

"She's not an it, she's a she, and Seraphina will last much longer than a car. She'll probably last longer than you will."

"But, Milly, your trips out to the stables, and the stabling alone . . ."

"I've talked about all that with Captain Segura. He's offering me a rock-bottom price. He wanted to give me free stabling, but I knew you wouldn't like me to take favours."

"Who's Captain Segura, Milly?"

"The head police officer in Vedado."

"Where on earth did you meet him?"

"Oh, he often gives me a lift to Lamparilla in his car."

"Does Reverend Mother know about this?"

Milly said stiffly, "One must have one's private life."

"Listen, Milly, I can't afford a horse, you can't afford

all this—stuff. You'll have to take it back." He added with fury, "And I won't have you taking lifts from Captain Segura."

"Don't worry. He never touches me," Milly said. "He only sings sad Mexican songs while he drives. About flowers and death. And one about a bull."

"I won't have it, Milly. I shall speak to Reverend Mother, you've got to promise . . ." He could see under the dark brows how the green and amber eyes contained the coming tears. Wormold felt the approach of panic; just so his wife had looked at him one blistering October afternoon when six years of life suddenly ended. He said, "You aren't in love, are you, with this Captain Segura?"

Two tears chased each other with a kind of elegance round the curve of a cheek-bone and glittered like the harness on the wall; they were part of her equipment too. "I don't care a damn about Captain Segura," Milly said. "It's just Seraphina I care about. She's fifteen hands and she's got a mouth like velvet, everybody says so."

"Milly dear, you know that if I could manage it . . ."

"Oh, I knew you'd take it like this," Milly said. "I knew it in my heart of hearts. I said two novenas to make it come right, but they haven't worked. I was so careful too. I was in a state of grace all the time I said them. I'll never believe in a novena again. Never. Never." Her voice had the lingering resonance of Poe's Raven. He had no faith himself, but he never wanted by any action of his own to weaken hers. Now he felt a fearful responsibility; at any moment she would be denying the existence of God. Ancient promises he had made came up out of the past to weaken him.

He said, "Milly, I'm sorry . . ."

"I've done two extra Masses as well." She shovelled on to his shoulders all her disappointment in the old familiar magic. It was all very well talking about the easy tears of a child, but if you are a father you can't take risks as a schoolteacher can or a governess. Who knows whether there may not be a moment in childhood when the world

changes for ever, like making a face when the clock
strikes?

"Milly, I promise if it's possible next year . . . Listen,
Milly, you can keep the saddle till then, and all the rest of
the stuff."

"What's the good of a saddle without a horse? And I
told Captain Segura . . ."

"Damn Captain Segura—what did you tell him?"

"I told him I had only to ask you for Seraphina and
you'd give her to me. I said you were wonderful. I didn't
tell him about the novenas."

"How much is she?"

"Three hundred pesos."

"Oh, Milly, Milly." There was nothing he could do
but surrender. "You'll have to pay out of your allowance
towards the stabling."

"Of course I will." She kissed his ear. "I'll start next
month." They both knew very well that she would never
start. She said, "You see, they did work after all, the
novenas, I mean. I'll begin another tomorrow, to make
business good. I wonder which saint is best for that."

"I've heard that St. Jude is the saint of lost causes,"
Wormold said.

[3]

i

It was Wormold's day-dream that he would wake some
day and find that he had amassed savings, bearer-bonds
and share-certificates, and that he was receiving a steady
flow of dividends like the rich inhabitants of the Vedado
suburb; then he would retire with Milly to England, where
there would be no Captain Seguras and no wolf-whistles.
But the dream faded whenever he entered the big American bank in Obispo. Passing through the great stone por-
tals, which were decorated with four-leaved clovers, he

became again the small dealer he really was, whose pension would never be sufficient to take Milly to the region of safety.

Drawing a cheque is not nearly so simple an operation in an American bank as in an English one. American bankers believe in the personal touch; the teller conveys a sense that he happens to be there accidentally and he is overjoyed at the lucky chance of the encounter. "Well," he seems to express in the sunny warmth of his smile, "who would have believed that I'd meet you here, you of all people, in a bank of all places?" After exchanging with him news of your health and of his health, and after finding a common interest in the fineness of the winter weather, you shyly, apologetically, slide the cheque towards him (how tiresome and incidental all such business is), but he barely has time to glance at it when the telephone rings at his elbow. "Why, Henry," he exclaims in astonishment over the telephone, as though Henry too were the last person he expected to speak to on such a day, "what's the news of you?" The news takes a long time to absorb; the teller smiles whimsically at you: business is business.

"I must say Edith was looking swell last night," the teller said.

Wormold shifted restlessly.

"It was a swell evening, it certainly was. Me? Oh, I'm fine. Well now, what can we do for you today?"

" . . . . "

"Why, anything to oblige, Henry, you know that . . . A hundred and fifty thousand dollars for three years . . . no, of course there won't be any difficulty for a business like yours. We have to get the O.K. from New York, but that's a formality. Just step in any time and talk to the manager. Monthly payments? That's not necessary with an American firm. I'd say we could arrange five per cent. Make it two hundred thousand for four years? Of course, Henry."

Wormold's cheque shrank to insignificance in his fingers. "Three hundred and fifty dollars"—the writing seemed to him almost as thin as his resources.

"See you at Mrs. Slater's tomorrow? I expect there'll be a rubber. Don't bring any aces up your sleeve, Henry. How long for the O.K.? Oh, a couple of days if we cable. Eleven tomorrow? Any time you say, Henry. Just walk in. I'll tell the manager. He'll be tickled to death to see you."

"Sorry to keep you waiting, Mr. Wormold." Surname again. Perhaps, Wormold thought, I am not worth cultivating or perhaps it is our nationalities that keep us apart. "Three hundred and fifty dollars?" The teller took an unobtrusive glance in a file before counting out the notes. He had hardly begun when the telephone rang a second time.

"Why, Mrs. Ashworth, where have you been hiding yourself? Over at Miami? No kidding?" It was several minutes before he had finished with Mrs. Ashworth. As he passed the notes to Wormold, he handed over a slip of paper as well. "You don't mind, do you, Mr. Wormold. You asked me to keep you informed." The slip showed an overdraft of fifty dollars.

"Not at all. It's very kind of you," Wormold said. "But there's nothing to worry about."

"Oh, the bank's not worrying, Mr. Wormold. You just asked, that's all."

Wormold thought, If the overdraft had been fifty thousand dollars he would have called me Jim.

ii

For some reason that morning he had no wish to meet Dr. Hasselbacher for his morning daiquiri. There were times when Dr. Hasselbacher was a little too carefree, so he looked in at Sloppy Joe's instead of at the Wonder Bar. No Havana resident ever went to Sloppy Joe's because it was the rendezvous of tourists; but tourists were sadly reduced nowadays in number, for the President's régime was creaking dangerously towards its end. There had always been unpleasant doings out of sight, in the inner rooms of the Jefatura, which had not disturbed the tourists in the Nacional and the Seville-Biltmore, but one tourist had recently been killed by a stray bullet while he was taking a photograph of a picturesque beggar under a balcony near the palace, and the death had sounded the knell of the all-in tour "including a trip to Varadero beach and the night-life of Havana." The victim's Leica had been smashed as well, and that had impressed his companions more than anything with the destructive power of a bullet. Wormold had heard them talking afterwards in the bar of the Nacional. "Ripped right through the camera," one of them said. "Five hundred dollars gone just like that."

"Was he killed at once?"

"Sure. And the lens—you could pick up bits for fifty yards around. Look, I'm taking a piece home to show Mr. Humpelnicker."

The long bar that morning was empty except for the elegant stranger at one end and a stout member of the tourist police who was smoking a cigar at the other. The Englishman was absorbed in the sight of so many bottles, and it was quite a while before he spotted Wormold. "Well I never," he said, "Mr. Wormold, isn't it?" Wormold wondered how he knew his name, for he had forgotten to give him a trade-card. "Eighteen different kinds of Scotch," the stranger said, "including Black Label. And I haven't counted the Bourbons. It's a wonderful sight. Wonderful," he repeated, lowering his voice with respect. "Have you ever seen so many whiskies?"

"As a matter of fact I have. I collect miniatures and I have ninety-nine at home."

"Interesting. And what's your choice today? A dimpled Haig?"

"Thanks, I've just ordered a daiquiri."

"Can't take those things. They relax me."

"Have you decided on a cleaner yet?" Wormold asked for the sake of conversation.

"Cleaner?"

"Vacuum cleaner. The things I sell."

"Oh, cleaner. Ha ha. Throw away that stuff and have a Scotch."

"I never drink Scotch before the evening."

"You Southerners!"

"I don't see the connexion."

"Makes the blood thin. Sun, I mean. You were born in Nice, weren't you?"

"How do you know that?"

"Oh well, one picks things up. Here and there. Talking to this chap and that. I've been meaning to have a word with you as a matter of fact."

"Well, here I am."

"I'd like it more on the quiet, you know. Chaps keep on coming in and out."

No description could have been less accurate. No one even passed the door in the hard straight sunlight outside. The officer of the tourist police had fallen contentedly asleep after propping his cigar over an ash-tray; there were no tourists at this hour to protect or to supervise. Wormold said, "If it's about a cleaner, come down to the shop."

"I'd rather not, you know. Don't want to be seen hanging about there. Bar's not a bad place after all. You run into a fellow-countryman, have a get together, what more natural?"

"I don't understand."

"Well, you know how it is."

"I don't."

"Well, wouldn't you say it was natural enough?"

Wormold gave up. He left eighty cents on the counter and said, "I must be getting back to the shop."

"Why?"

"I don't like to leave Lopez for long."

"Ah, Lopez. I want to talk to you about Lopez." Again the explanation that seemed most probable to Wormold was that the stranger was an eccentric inspector from headquarters, but surely he had reached the limit of eccentricity when he added in a low voice, "You go to the Gents and I'll follow you."

"The Gents? Why should I?"

"Because I don't know the way."

In a mad world it always seems simpler to obey. Wormold led the stranger through a door at the back, down a short passage, and indicated the toilet. "It's in there."

"After you, old man."

"But I don't need it."

"Don't be difficult," the stranger said. He put a hand on Wormold's shoulder and pushed him through the door. Inside there were two wash-basins, a chair with a broken back, and the usual cabinets and pissoirs. "Take a pew, old man," the stranger said, "while I turn on a tap." But when the water ran he made no attempt to wash. "Looks more natural," he explained (the word "natural" seemed a favourite adjective of his), "if someone barges in. And of course it confuses a mike."

"A mike?"

"You're quite right to question that. Quite right. There probably wouldn't be a mike in a place like this, but it's the drill, you know, that counts. You'll find it always pays in the end to follow the drill. It's lucky they don't run to waste-plugs in Havana. We can just keep the water running."

"Please will you explain . . . ?"

"Can't be too careful even in a Gents, when I come to think of it. A chap of ours in Denmark in 1940 saw from his own window the German fleet coming down the Kattegat."

"What gut?"

"Kattegat. Of course he knew then the balloon had gone up. Started burning his papers. Put the ashes down the lav. and pulled the chain. Trouble was—late frost. Pipes frozen. All the ashes floated up into the bath down below. Flat belonged to an old maiden lady—Baronin someone or other. She was just going to have a bath. Most embarrassing for our chap."

"It sounds like the Secret Service."

"It *is* the Secret Service, old man, or so the novelists call it. That's why I wanted to talk to you about your chap Lopez. Is he reliable or ought you to fire him?"

"Are you in the Secret Service?"

"If you like to put it that way."

"Why on earth should I fire Lopez? He's been with me ten years."

"We could find you a chap who knew all about vacuum cleaners. But of course—naturally—we'll leave that decision to you."

"But I'm not in your Service."

"We'll come to that in a moment, old man. Anyway we've traced Lopez—he seems clear. But your friend Hasselbacher, I'd be a bit careful of him."

"How do you know about Hasselbacher?"

"I've been around a day or two, picking things up. One has to on these occasions."

"What occasions?"

"Where was Hasselbacher born?"

"Berlin, I think."

"Sympathies East or West?"

"We never talk politics."

"Not that it matters—East or West they play the German game. Remember the Ribbentrop Pact. We won't be caught that way again."

"Hasselbacher's not a politician. He's an old doctor and he's lived here for thirty years."

"All the same, you'd be surprised . . . But I agree with you, it would be conspicuous if you dropped him. Just play him carefully, that's all. He might even be useful if you handle him right."

"I've no intention of handling him."

"You'll find it necessary for the job."

"I don't want any job. Why do you pick on me?"

"Patriotic Englishman. Been here for years. Respected member of the European Traders' Association. We must have our man in Havana, you know. Submarines need fuel. Dictators drift together. Big ones draw in the little ones."

"Atomic submarines don't need fuel."

"Quite right, old man, quite right. But wars always start a little behind the times. Have to be prepared for conventional weapons too. Then there's economic intelligence—sugar, coffee, tobacco."

"You can find all that in the Government year-books."

"We don't trust them, old man. Then political intelligence. With your cleaners you've got the entrée everywhere."

"Do you expect me to analyse the fluff?"

"It may seem a joke to you, old man, but the main source of the French intelligence at the time of Dreyfus was a charwoman who collected the scraps out of the waste-paper baskets at the German Embassy."

"I don't even know your name."

"Hawthorne."

"But who are you?"

"Well, you might say I'm setting up the Caribbean network. One moment. Someone's coming. I'll wash. You slip into a closet. Mustn't be seen together."

"We *have* been seen together."

"Passing encounter. Fellow-countrymen." He thrust Wormold into the compartment as he had thrust him into the lavatory, "It's the drill, you know," and then there was silence except for the running tap. Wormold sat down. There was nothing else to do. When he was seated his legs still showed under the half door. A handle turned. Feet crossed the tiled floor towards the pissoir. Water went on running. Wormold felt an enormous bewilderment. He wondered why he had not stopped all this nonsense at the beginning. No wonder Mary had left him. He remembered one of their quarrels. "Why don't you do something, act some way, any way at all? You just stand there . . ." At least, he thought, this time I'm not standing, I'm sitting. But in any case what could he have said? He hadn't been given time to get a word in. Minutes passed. What enormous bladders Cubans had, and how clean Hawthorne's hands must be getting by this time. The water stopped running. Presumably he was drying his hands, but Wormold remembered there were no towels. That was another problem for Hawthorne, but he would be up to it. All part of the drill. At last the feet passed towards the door. The door closed.

"Can I come out?" Wormold asked. It was like a surrender. He was under orders now.

He heard Hawthorne tiptoeing near. "Give me a few minutes to get away, old man. Do you know who that was? The policeman. A bit suspicious, eh?"

"He may have recognised my legs under the door. Do you think we ought to change trousers?"

"Wouldn't look natural," Hawthorne said, "but you are getting the idea. I'm leaving the key of my room in the basin. Fifth floor Seville-Biltmore. Just walk up. Ten tonight. Things to discuss. Money and so on. Sordid issues. Don't ask for me at the desk."

"Don't you need your key?"

"Got a pass key. I'll be seeing you."

Wormold stood up in time to see the door close behind the elegant figure and the appalling slang. The key was there in the wash-basin—Room 501.

iii

At half-past nine Wormold went to Milly's room to say good night. Here, where the duenna was in charge, everything was in order—the candle had been lit before the statue of St. Seraphina, the honey-coloured missal lay beside the bed, the clothes were eliminated as though they had never existed, and a faint smell of eau-de-Cologne blew about like incense.

"You've got something on your mind," Milly said. "You aren't still worrying, are you, about Captain Segura?"

"You never pull my leg, do you, Milly?"

"No. Why?"

"Everybody else seems to."

"Did Mother?"

"I suppose so. In the early days."

"Does Dr. Hasselbacher?"

He remembered the negro limping slowly by. He said, "Perhaps. Sometimes."

"It's a sign of affection, isn't it?"

"Not always. I remember at school——" He stopped.

"What do you remember, Father?"

"Oh, a lot of things."

Childhood was the germ of all mistrust. You were cruelly joked upon and then you cruelly joked. You lost the remembrance of pain through inflicting it. But somehow, through no virtue of his own, he had never taken that course. Lack of character perhaps. Schools were said to construct character by chipping off the edges. His edges had been chipped, but the result had not, he thought, been character—only shapelessness, like an exhibit in the Museum of Modern Art.

"Are you happy, Milly?" he asked.

"Oh yes."

"At school too?"

"Yes. Why?"

"Nobody pulls your hair now?"

"Of course not."

"And you don't set anyone on fire?"

"That was when I was thirteen," she said with scorn. "What's worrying you, Father?"

She sat up in bed, wearing a white nylon dressing-gown. He loved her when the duenna was there, and he loved her even more when the duenna was absent: he couldn't afford the time not to love. It was as if he had come with her a little way on a journey that she would finish alone. The separating years approached them both, like a station down the line, all gain for her and all loss for him. That evening hour was real, but not Hawthorne, mysterious and absurd, not the cruelties of police-stations and governments, the scientists who tested the new H-bomb on Christmas Island, Khrushchev who wrote notes: these seemed less real to him than the inefficient tortures of a school-dormitory. The small boy with the damp towel whom he had just remembered—where was he now? The cruel come and go like cities and thrones and powers, leaving their ruins behind them. They had no permanence. But the clown whom he had seen last year with Milly at the circus—that clown was permanent, for his act never changed. That was the way to live; the clown was unaffected by the vagaries of public men and the enormous discoveries of the great.

Wormold began to make faces in the glass.

"What on earth are you doing, Father?"

"I wanted to make myself laugh."

Milly giggled. "I thought you were being sad and serious."

"That's why I wanted to laugh. Do you remember the clown last year, Milly?"

"He walked off the end of a ladder and fell in a bucket of whitewash."

"He falls in it every night at ten o'clock. We should all be clowns, Milly. Don't ever learn from experience."

"Reverend Mother says . . ."

"Don't pay any attention to her. God doesn't learn from experience, does He, or how could He hope anything of man? It's the scientists who add the digits and make the same sum who cause the trouble. Newton discovering gravity—he learned from experience and after that . . ."

"I thought it was from an apple."

"It's the same thing. It was only a matter of time before Lord Rutherford went and split the atom. He had learned from experience too, and so did the men of Hiroshima. If only we had been born clowns, nothing bad would happen to us except a few bruises and a smear of whitewash. Don't learn from experience, Milly. It ruins our peace and our lives."

"What are you doing now?"

"I'm trying to waggle my ears. I used to be able to do it. But the trick doesn't work any longer."

"Are you still unhappy about Mother?"

"Sometimes."

"Are you still in love with her?"

"Perhaps. Now and then."

"I suppose she was very beautiful when she was young."

"She can't be old now. Thirty-six."

"That's pretty old."

"Don't you remember her at all?"

"Not very well. She was away a lot, wasn't she?"

"A good deal."

"Of course I pray for her."

"What do you pray? That she'll come back?"

"Oh no, not *that*. We can do without her. I pray that she'll be a good Catholic again."

"I'm not a good Catholic."

"Oh, that's different. You are invincibly ignorant."

"Yes, I expect I am."

"I'm not insulting you, Father. It's only theology. You'll be saved like the good pagans. Socrates, you know, and Cetewayo."

"Who was Cetewayo?"

"He was king of the Zulus."

"What else do you pray?"

"Well, of course, lately I've been concentrating on the horse."

He kissed her good night. She asked, "Where are you going?"

"There are things I've got to arrange about the horse."

"I give you a lot of trouble," she said meaninglessly. Then she sighed with content, pulling the sheet up to her neck. "It's wonderful, isn't it, how you always get what you pray for."

[4]

i

At every corner there were men who called "Taxi" at him as though he were a stranger, and all down the Paseo, at intervals of a few yards, the pimps accosted him automatically without any real hope. "Can I be of service, sir?" "I know all the pretty girls." "You desire a beautiful woman." "Postcards?" "You want to see a dirty movie?"

They had been mere children when he first came to Havana, they had watched his car for a nickel, and though they had aged alongside him they had never got used to him. In their eyes he never became a resident; he remained a permanent tourist, and so they went pegging along—sooner or later, like all the others, they were certain that he would want to see Superman performing at the San Francisco brothel. At least, like the clown, they had the comfort of not learning from experience.

By the corner of Virdudes Dr. Hasselbacher hailed him from the Wonder Bar. "Mr. Wormold, where are you off to in such a hurry?"

"An appointment."

"There is always time for a Scotch." It was obvious from the way he pronounced Scotch that Dr. Hasselbacher had already had time for a great many.

"I'm late as it is."

"There's no such thing as late in this city, Mr. Wormold. And I have a present for you."

Wormold turned in to the bar from the Paseo. He smiled unhappily at one of his own thoughts. "Are your sympathies with the East or the West, Hasselbacher?"

"East or West of what? Oh, you mean *that*. A plague on both."

"What present have you got for me?"

"I asked one of my patients to bring them from Miami," Hasselbacher said. He took from his pocket two miniature bottles of whisky: one was Lord Calvert, the other Old Taylor. "Have you got them?" he asked with anxiety.

"I've got the Calvert, but not the Taylor. It was kind of you to remember my collection, Hasselbacher." It always seemed strange to Wormold that he continued to exist for others when he was not there.

"How many have you got now?"

"A hundred with the Bourbon and the Irish. Seventy-six Scotch."

"When are you going to drink them?"

"Perhaps when they reach two hundred."

"Do you know what I'd do with them if I were you?"

Hasselbacher said. "Play checkers. When you take a piece you drink it."

"That's quite an idea."

"A natural handicap," Hasselbacher said. "That's the beauty of it. The better player has to drink more. Think of the finesse. Have another Scotch."

"Perhaps I will."

"I need your help. I was stung by a wasp this morning."

"You are the doctor, not me."

"That's not the point. One hour later, going out on a sick call beyond the airport, I ran over a chicken."

"I still don't understand."

"Mr. Wormold, Mr. Wormold, your thoughts are far away. Come back to earth. We have to find a lottery-ticket at once, before the draw. Twenty-seven means a wasp. Thirty-seven a chicken."

"But I have an appointment."

"Appointments can wait. Drink down that Scotch. We've got to hunt for the ticket in the market." Wormold followed him to his car. Like Milly, Dr. Hasselbacher had faith. He was controlled by numbers as she was by saints.

All round the market hung the important numbers in blue and red. What were called the ugly numbers lay under the counter; they were left for the small fry and the street sellers to dispose of. They were without importance, they contained no significant figure, no number that represented a nun or a cat, a wasp or a chicken. "Look. There's 2 7 4 8 3," Wormold pointed out.

"A wasp is no good without a chicken," said Dr. Hasselbacher. They parked the car and walked. There were no pimps around this market; the lottery was a serious trade uncorrupted by tourists. Once a week the numbers were distributed by a government department, and a politician would be allotted tickets according to the value of his support. He paid $18 a ticket to the department and he resold to the big merchants for $21. Even if his share were a mere twenty tickets he could depend on a profit of sixty dollars a week. A beautiful number

containing omens of a popular kind could be sold by the
merchants for anything up to thirty dollars. No such
profits, of course, were possible for the little man in the
street. With only ugly numbers, for which he had paid as
much as twenty-three dollars, he really had to work for a
living. He would divide a ticket up into a hundred parts
at twenty-five cents a part; he would haunt car parks until
he found a car with the same number as one of his tickets
(no owner could resist a coincidence like that); he would
even search for his numbers in the telephone-book and
risk a nickel on a call. "Señora, I have a lottery-ticket for
sale which is the same number as your telephone."

Wormold said, "Look, there's a 37 with a 72."

"Not good enough," Dr. Hasselbacher flatly replied.

Dr. Hasselbacher thumbed through the sheets of numbers which were not considered beautiful enough to be
displayed. One never knew; beauty was not beauty to all
men—there might be some to whom a wasp was insignifi-
cant. A police siren came shrieking through the dark
round three sides of the market, a car rocked by. A man
sat on the kerb with a single number displayed on his
shirt like a convict. He said, "The Red Vulture."

"Who's the Red Vulture?"

"Captain Segura, of course," Dr. Hasselbacher said.
"What a sheltered life you lead."

"Why do they call him that?"

"He specialises in torture and mutilation."

"Torture?"

"There's nothing here," Dr. Hasselbacher said. "We'd
better try Obispo."

"Why not wait till the morning?"

"Last day before the draw. Besides, what kind of cold
blood runs in your veins, Mr. Wormold? When fate
gives you a lead like this one—a wasp and a chicken—
you have to follow it without delay. One must deserve
one's good fortune."

They climbed back into the car and made for Obispo.
"This Captain Segura"—Wormold began.

"Yes?"

"Nothing."

It was eleven o'clock before they found a ticket that satisfied Dr. Hasselbacher's requirements, and then as the shop which displayed it was closed until the morning there was nothing to do but have another drink. "Where is your appointment?"

Wormold said, "The Seville-Biltmore."

"One place is as good as another," Dr. Hasselbacher said.

"Don't you think the Wonder Bar . . . ?"

"No, no. A change will be good. When you feel unable to change your bar you have become old."

They groped their way through the darkness of the Seville-Biltmore bar. They were only dimly aware of their fellow-guests, who sat crouched in silence and shadow like parachutists gloomily waiting the signal to leap. Only the high proof of Dr. Hasselbacher's spirits could not be quenched.

"You haven't won yet," Wormold whispered, trying to check him, but even a whisper caused a reproachful head to turn towards them in the darkness.

"Tonight I have won," Dr. Hasselbacher said in a loud firm voice. "Tomorrow I may have lost, but nothing can rob me of my victory tonight. A hundred and forty thousand dollars, Mr. Wormold. It is a pity that I am too old for women—I could have made a beautiful woman very happy with a necklace of rubies. Now I am at a loss. How shall I spend my money, Mr. Wormold? Endow a hospital?"

"Pardon me," a voice whispered out of the shadows, "has this guy really won a hundred and forty thousand bucks?"

"Yes, sir, I have won them," Dr. Hasselbacher said firmly before Wormold could reply, "I have won them as certainly as you exist, my almost unseen friend. You would not exist if I didn't believe you existed, nor would those dollars. I believe, therefore you are."

"What do you mean I wouldn't exist?"

"You exist only in my thoughts, my friend. If I left this room . . ."

"You're nuts."

"Prove you exist, then."

"What do you mean, prove? Of course I exist. I've got a first-class business in real estate: a wife and a couple of kids in Miami: I flew here this morning by Delta: I'm drinking this Scotch, aren't I?" The voice contained a hint of tears.

"Poor fellow," Dr. Hasselbacher said, "you deserve a more imaginative creator than I have been. Why didn't I do better for you than Miami and real estate? Something of imagination. A name to be remembered."

"What's wrong with my name?"

The parachutists at both ends of the bar were tense with disapproval; one shouldn't show nerves before the jump.

"Nothing that I cannot remedy by taking a little thought."

"You ask anyone in Miami about Harry Morgan . . ."

"I really should have done better than that. But I'll tell you what I'll do," Dr. Hasselbacher said, "I'll go out of the bar for a minute and eliminate you. Then I'll come back with an improved version."

"What do you mean, an improved version?"

"Now if my friend, Mr. Wormold here, had invented you, you would have been a happier man. He would have given you an Oxford education, a name like Pennyfeather . . ."

"What do you mean, Pennyfeather? You've been drinking."

"Of course I've been drinking. Drink blurs the imagination. That's why I thought you up in so banal a way: Miami and real estate, flying Delta. Pennyfeather would have come from Europe by K.L.M., he would be drinking his national drink, a pink gin."

"I'm drinking Scotch and I like it."

"You think you're drinking Scotch. Or rather, to be accurate, I have imagined you drinking Scotch. But we're going to change all that," Dr. Hasselbacher said cheerily. "I'll just go out in the hall for a minute and think up some real improvements."

"You can't monkey around with me," the man said with anxiety.

Dr. Hasselbacher drained his drink, laid a dollar on the bar, and rose with uncertain dignity. "You'll thank me for this," he said. "What shall it be? Trust me and Mr. Wormold here. A painter, a poet—or would you prefer a life of adventure, a gun-runner, a Secret Service agent?"

He bowed from the doorway to the agitated shadow. "I apologise for the real estate."

The voice said nervously, seeking reassurance, "He's drunk or nuts," but the parachutists made no reply.

Wormold said, "Well, I'll be saying good night, Hasselbacher. I'm late."

"The least I can do, Mr. Wormold, is to accompany you and explain how I came to delay you. I'm sure when I tell your friend of my good fortune he will understand."

"It's not necessary. It's really not necessary," Wormold said. Hawthorne, he knew, would jump to conclusions. A reasonable Hawthorne, if such existed, was bad enough, but a suspicious Hawthorne . . . His mind boggled at the thought.

He made towards the lift with Dr. Hasselbacher trailing behind. Ignoring a red signal light and a warning "Mind the Step," Dr. Hasselbacher stumbled. "Oh dear," he said, "my ankle."

"Go home, Hasselbacher," Wormold said with desperation. He stepped into the lift, but Dr. Hasselbacher, putting on a turn of speed, entered too. He said, "There's no pain that money won't cure. It's a long time since I've had such a good evening."

"Sixth floor," Wormold said. "I want to be alone, Hasselbacher."

"Why? Excuse me. I have the hiccups."

"This is a private meeting."

"A lovely woman, Mr. Wormold? You shall have some of my winnings to help you stoop to folly."

"Of course it isn't a woman. It's business, that's all."

"Private business?"

"I told you so."

"What can be so private about a vacuum cleaner, Mr. Wormold?"

"A new agency," Wormold said, and the liftman announced, "Sixth floor."

Wormold was a length ahead and his brain was clearer than Hasselbacher's. The rooms were built as prison-cells round a rectangular balcony; on the ground floor two bald heads gleamed upwards like traffic globes. He limped to the corner of the balcony where the stairs were, and Dr. Hasselbacher limped after him but Wormold was practised in limping. "Mr. Wormold." Dr. Hasselbacher called, "Mr. Wormold, I'd be happy to invest a hundred thousand of my dollars . . ."

Wormold got to the bottom of the stairs while Dr. Hasselbacher was still manœuvring the first step; 501 was close by. He unlocked the door. A small table-lamp showed him an empty sitting-room. He closed the door very softly—Dr. Hasselbacher had not yet reached the bottom of the stairs. He stood listening and heard Dr. Hasselbacher's hop, skip and hiccup pass the door and recede. Wormold thought, I feel like a spy, I behave like a spy. This is absurd. What am I going to say to Hasselbacher in the morning?

The bedroom door was closed and he began to move towards it. Then he stopped. Let sleeping dogs lie. If Hawthorne wanted him, let Hawthorne find him without his stirring, but a curiosity about Hawthorne induced him to make a parting examination of the room.

On the writing desk were two books—identical copies of Lamb's *Tales from Shakespeare*. A memo pad—on which perhaps Hawthorne had made notes for their meeting—read, "1. Salary. 2. Expenses. 3. Transmission. 4. Charles Lamb. 5. Ink." He was just about to open the Lamb when a voice said, "Put up your hands. *Arriba los manos.*"

"*Las manos,*" Wormold corrected him. He was relieved to see that it was Hawthorne.

"Oh, it's only you," Hawthorne said.

"I'm a bit late. I'm sorry. I was out with Hasselbacher."

Hawthorne was wearing mauve silk pyjamas with a monogram H.R.H. on the pocket. This gave him a royal air. He said, "I fell asleep and then I heard you moving around." It was as though he had been caught without his slang; he hadn't yet had time to put it on with his clothes. He said, "You've moved the Lamb," accusingly as though he were in charge of a Salvation Army chapel.

"I'm sorry. I was just looking round."

"Never mind. It shows you have the right instinct."

"You seem fond of that particular book."

"One copy is for you."

"But I've read it," Wormold said, "years ago, and I don't like Lamb."

"It's not meant for reading. Have you never heard of a book-code?"

"As a matter of fact—no."

"In a minute I'll show you how to work it. I keep one copy. All you have to do when you communicate with me is to indicate the page and line where you begin the coding. Of course it's not so hard to break as a machine-code, but it's hard enough for the mere Hasselbachers."

"I wish you'd get Dr. Hasselbacher out of your head."

"When we have your office here properly organised with sufficient security—a combination-safe, radio, trained staff, all the gimmicks, then of course we can abandon a primitive code like this, but except for an expert cryptologist it's damned hard to break without knowing the name and edition of the book."

"Why did you choose Lamb?"

"It was the only book I could find in duplicate except *Uncle Tom's Cabin*. I was in a hurry and had to get something at the C.T.S. bookshop in Kingston before I left. Oh, there was something too called *The Lit Lamp: A Manual of Evening Devotion,* but I thought somehow it might look conspicuous on your shelves if you weren't a religious man."

"I'm not."

"I brought you some ink as well. Have you got an electric kettle?"

"Yes. Why?"

"For opening letters. We like our men to be equipped against an emergency."

"What's the ink for? I've got plenty of ink at home."

"Secret ink of course. In case you have to send anything by the ordinary mail. Your daughter has a knitting needle, I suppose?"

"She doesn't knit."

"Then you'll have to buy one. Plastic is best. Steel sometimes leaves a mark."

"Mark where?"

"On the envelopes you open."

"Why on earth should I want to open envelopes?"

"It might be necessary for you to examine Dr. Hasselbacher's mail. Of course, you'll have to find a sub-agent in the post office."

"I absolutely refuse . . ."

"Don't be difficult. I'm having traces of him sent out from London. We'll decide about his mail after we've read them. A good tip—if you run short of ink use bird shit, or am I going too fast?"

"I haven't even said I was willing . . ."

"London agrees to $150 a month, with another hundred and fifty as expenses—you'll have to justify those, of course. Payment of sub-agents, etc. Anything above that will have to be specially authorised."

"You are going much too fast."

"Free of income-tax, you know," Hawthorne said and winked slyly. The wink somehow didn't go with the royal monogram.

"You must give me time . . ."

"Your code number is 59200 stroke 5." He added with pride, "Of course *I* am 59200. You'll number your sub-agents 59200 stroke 5 stroke 1 and so on. Got the idea?"

"I don't see how I can possibly be of use to you."

"You are English, aren't you?" Hawthorne said briskly.

"Of course I'm English."

"And you refuse to serve your country?"

"I didn't say that. But the vacuum cleaners take up a great deal of time."

"They are an excellent cover," Hawthorne said. "Very well thought out. Your profession has quite a natural air."

"But it *is* natural."

"Now if you don't mind," Hawthorne said firmly, "we must get down to our Lamb."

ii

"Milly," Wormold said, "you haven't taken any cereals."

"I've given up cereals."

"You only took one lump of sugar in your coffee. You aren't going on a diet, are you?"

"No."

"Or doing a penance?"

"No."

"You'll be awfully hungry by lunch-time."

"I've thought of that. I'm going to eat a terrible lot of potatoes."

"Milly, what's going on?"

"I'm going to economise. Suddenly in the watches of the night I realised what an expense I was to you. It was like a voice speaking. I nearly said, 'Who are you?' but I was afraid it would say, 'Your Lord and your God.' I'm about the age, you know."

"Age for what?"

"Voices. I'm older than St. Thérèse was when she went into the convent."

"Now, Milly, don't tell me you're contemplating . . ."

"No, I'm not. I think Captain Segura's right. He said I wasn't the right material for a convent."

"Milly, do you know what they call your Captain Segura?"

"Yes. The Red Vulture. He tortures prisoners."

"Does he admit that?"

"Oh, of course with me he's on his best behaviour, but he has a cigarette-case made out of human skin. He pretends it's calf—as if I didn't know calf when I see it."

"You must drop him, Milly."

"I shall—slowly, but I have to arrange my stabling first. And that reminds me of the voice."

"What did the voice say?"

"It said—only it sounded much more apocalyptic in the middle of the night—'You've bitten off more than you can chew, my girl. What about the Country Club?'"

"What about the Country Club?"

"It's the only place where I can get any real riding, and we aren't members. What's the good of a horse in a stable? Of course Captain Segura is a member, but I knew you wouldn't want me to depend on him. So I thought perhaps if I could help you to cut the housekeeping by fasting . . ."

"What good . . . ?"

"Well, then, you might be able to afford to take a family-membership. You ought to enter me as Seraphina. It somehow sounds more suitable than Milly."

It seemed to Wormold that all she said had a quality of sense; it was Hawthorne who belonged to the cruel and inexplicable world of childhood.

Interlude in London

In the basement of the big steel and concrete building near Maida Vale a light over a door changed from red to green, and Hawthorne entered. He had left his elegance behind in the Caribbean and wore a grey flannel suit which had seen better days. At home he didn't have to keep up appearances; he was part of grey January London.

The Chief sat behind a desk on which an enormous green marble paper-weight held down a single sheet of paper. A half-drunk glass of milk, a bottle of grey pills and a packet of Kleenex stood by the black telephone.

(The red one was for scrambling.) His black morning coat, black tie and black monocle hiding the left eye gave him the appearance of an undertaker, just as the basement room had the effect of a vault, a mausoleum, a grave.

"You wanted me, sir?"

"Just a gossip, Hawthorne. Just a gossip." It was as though a mute were gloomily giving tongue after the day's burials were over. "When did you get back, Hawthorne?"

"A week ago, sir. I'll be returning to Jamaica on Friday."

"All going well?"

"I think we've got the Caribbean sewn up now, sir," Hawthorne said.

"Martinique?"

"No difficulties there, sir. You remember at Fort de France we are working with the Deuxième Bureau."

"Only up to a point?"

"Oh yes, of course, only up to a point. Haiti was more of a problem, but 59200 stroke 2 is proving energetic. I was more uncertain at first about 59200 stroke 5."

"Stroke five?"

"Our man in Havana, sir. I didn't have much choice there, and at first he didn't seem very keen on the job. A bit stubborn."

"That kind sometimes develops best."

"Yes, sir. I was a little worried too by his contacts. (There's a German called Hasselbacher, but we haven't found any traces of him yet.) However he seems to be going ahead. We got a request for extra expenses just as I was leaving Kingston."

"Always a good sign."

"Yes, sir."

"Shows the imagination is working."

"Yes. He wanted to become a member of the Country Club. Haunt of the millionaires, you know. Best source for political and economic information. The subscription's very high, about ten times the size of White's, but I've allowed it."

"You did right. How are his reports?"

"Well, as a matter of fact, we haven't had any yet, but of course it will take time for him to organise his contacts. Perhaps I rather over-emphasised the need of security."

"You can't. No use having a live wire if it fuses."

"As it happens, he's rather advantageously placed. Very good business contacts—a lot of them with Government officials and leading Ministers."

"Ah," the Chief said. He took off the black monocle and began to polish it with a piece of Kleenex. The eye that he disclosed was made of glass; pale blue and unconvincing, it might have come out of a doll which said "Mama."

"What's his business?"

"Oh, he imports, you know. Machinery, that sort of thing." It was always important to one's own career to employ agents who were men of good social standing. The petty details on the secret file dealing with the store in Lamparilla Street would never, in ordinary circumstances, reach this basement-room.

"Why isn't he already a member of the Country Club?"

"Well, I think he's been rather a recluse of recent years. Bit of domestic trouble."

"Doesn't run after women, I hope?"

"Oh, nothing of that sort, sir. His wife left him. Went off with an American."

"I suppose he's not anti-American? Havana's not the place for any prejudice like that. We have to work with them—only up to a point of course."

"Oh, he's not at all that way, sir. He's a very fair-minded man, very balanced. Took his divorce well and keeps his child in a Catholic school according to his wife's wishes. I'm told he sends her greeting-telegrams at Christmas. I think we'll find his reports when they do come in are a hundred per cent reliable."

"Rather touching that, about the child, Hawthorne. Well, give him a prod, so that we can judge his usefulness. If he's all you say he is, we might consider enlarging his staff. Havana could be a key-spot. The Communists always go where there's trouble. How does he communicate?"

"I've arranged for him to send reports by the weekly bag to Kingston in duplicate. I keep one and send one to London. I've given him the book-code for cables. He sends them through the Consulate."

"They won't like that."

"I've told them it's temporary."

"I would be in favour of establishing a radio-unit if he proves to be a good man. He could expand his office-staff, I suppose?"

"Oh, of course. At least—you understand it's not a big office, sir. Old-fashioned. You know how these merchant-adventurers make do."

"I know the type, Hawthorne. Small scrubby desk. Half a dozen men in an outer office meant to hold two. Out-of-date accounting machines. Woman-secretary who is completing forty years with the firm."

Hawthorne now felt able to relax; the Chief had taken charge. Even if one day he read the secret file, the words would convey nothing to him. The small shop for vacuum cleaners had been drowned beyond recovery in the tide of the Chief's literary imagination. Agent 59200/5 was established.

"It's all part of the man's character," the Chief explained to Hawthorne, as though he and not Hawthorne had pushed open the door in Lamparilla Street. "A man who has always learnt to count the pennies and to risk the pounds. That's why he's not a member of the Country Club—nothing to do with the broken marriage. You're a romantic, Hawthorne. Women have come and gone in his life; I suspect they never meant as much to him as his work. The secret of successfully using an agent is to understand him. Our man in Havana belongs—you might say—to the Kipling age. Walking with kings—how does it go?—and keeping your virtue, crowds and the common touch. I expect somewhere in that ink-stained desk of his there's an old penny note-book of black wash-leather in which he kept his first accounts—a quarter gross of india-rubbers, six boxes of steel nibs . . ."

"I don't think he goes quite as far back as steel nibs, sir."

The Chief sighed and replaced the black lens. The innocent eye had gone back into hiding at the hint of opposition.

"Details don't matter, Hawthorne," the Chief said with irritation. "But if you are to handle him successfully you'll have to find that penny note-book. I speak metaphorically."

"Yes, sir."

"This business about being a recluse because he lost his wife—it's a wrong appreciation, Hawthorne. A man like that reacts quite differently. He doesn't show his loss, he doesn't wear his heart on his sleeve. If your appreciation were correct, why wasn't he **a** member of the club before his wife died?"

"She left him."

"Left him? Are you sure?"

"Quite sure, sir."

"Ah, she never found that penny note-book. Find it, Hawthorne, and he's yours for life. What were we talking about?"

"The size of his office, sir. It won't be very easy for him to absorb many in the way of new staff."

"We'll weed out the old ones gradually. Pension off that old secretary of his . . ."

"As a matter of fact . . ."

"Of course this is just speculation, Hawthorne. He may not be the right man after all. Sterling stuff, these old merchant-kings, but sometimes they can't see far enough beyond the counting-house to be of use to people like ourselves. We'll judge by his first reports, but it's always well to plan a step ahead. Have a word with Miss Jenkinson and see if she has a Spanish speaker in her pool."

Hawthorne rose in the elevator floor by floor from the basement: a rocket's-eye view of the world. Western Europe sank below him: the Near East: Latin America. The filing cabinets stood around Miss Jenkinson like the pillars of a temple round an ageing oracle. She alone was known by her surname. For some inscrutable reason of security every other inhabitant in the building went by a Christian name. She was dictating to a secretary when Hawthorne entered, "Memo to A.O. Angelica has been transferred to C.5 with an increase of salary to £8 a week. Please see that this increase goes through at once. To anticipate your objections I would point out that Angelica is now approaching the financial level of a bus-conductress."

"Yes?" Miss Jenkinson asked sharply. "Yes?"

"The Chief told me to see you."

"I have nobody to spare."

"We don't want anybody at the moment. We're just discussing possibilities."

"Ethel, dear, telephone to D.2 and say I will not have my secretaries kept after 7 p.m. except in a national emergency. If a war has broken out or is likely to break out, say that the secretaries' pool should have been informed."

"We may be needing a Spanish-speaking secretary in the Caribbean."

"There's no one I can spare," Miss Jenkinson said mechanically.

"Havana—a small station, agreeable climate."

"How big is the staff?"

"At present one man."

"I'm not a marriage bureau," Miss Jenkinson said.

"A middle-aged man with a child of sixteen."

"Married?"

"You could call him that," Hawthorne said vaguely.

"Is he stable?"

"Stable?"

"Reliable, safe, emotionally secure?"

"Oh yes, yes, you may be certain of that. He's one of those old-fashioned merchant-types," Hawthorne said, picking up where the Chief had left off. "Built up the business from nothing. Uninterested in women. You might say he'd gone beyond sex."

"No one goes beyond sex," Miss Jenkinson said. "I'm responsible for the girls I send abroad."

"I thought you had nobody available."

"Well," Miss Jenkinson said, "I might possibly, under certain circumstances, let you have Beatrice."

"Beatrice, Miss Jenkinson!" a voice exclaimed from behind the filing cabinets.

"I said Beatrice, Ethel, and I mean Beatrice."

"But, Miss Jenkinson . . ."

"Beatrice needs some practical experience—that is really all that is amiss. The post would suit her. She is not too young. She is fond of children."

"What this station will need," Hawthorne said, "is someone who speaks Spanish. The love of children is not essential."

"Beatrice is half-French. She speaks French really better than she does English."

"I said Spanish."

"It's much the same. They're both Latin tongues."

"Perhaps I could see her, have a word with her. Is she fully trained?"

"She's a very good encoder and she's finished a course in microphotography at Ashley Park. Her shorthand is weak, but her typewriting is excellent. She has a good knowledge of electro-dynamics."

"What's that?"

"I'm not sure, but a fuse box holds no terrors for her."

"She'd be good with vacuum cleaners then?"

"She's a secretary, not a domestic help."

A file drawer slammed shut. "Take her or leave her," Miss Jenkinson said. Hawthorne had the impression that she would willingly have referred to Beatrice as "it."

"She's the only one you can suggest?"

"The only one."

Again a file drawer was noisily closed. "Ethel," Miss Jenkinson said, "unless you can relieve your feelings more silently, I shall return you to D.3."

Hawthorne went thoughtfully away; he had the impression that Miss Jenkinson with considerable agility had sold him something she didn't herself believe in—a gold brick or a small dog—bitch, rather.

PART II

[1]

i

Wormold came away from the Consulate Department carrying a cable in his breast-pocket. It had been shovelled rudely at him, and when he tried to speak he had been checked. "We don't want to know anything about it. A temporary arrangement. The sooner it's over the better we shall be pleased."

"Mr. Hawthorne said . . ."

"We don't know any Mr. Hawthorne. Please bear that in mind. Nobody of the name is employed here. Good morning."

He walked home. The long city lay spread along the open Atlantic; waves broke over the Avenida de Maceo and misted the windscreens of cars. The pink, grey, yellow pillars of what had once been the aristocratic quarter were eroded like rocks; an ancient coat of arms, smudged and featureless, was set over the doorway of a shabby hotel, and the shutters of a night-club were varnished in bright crude colours to protect them from the wet and salt of the sea. In the west the steel skyscrapers of the new town rose higher than lighthouses into the clear February sky. It was a city to visit, not a city to live in, but it was the city where Wormold had first fallen in love and he was held to it as though to the scene of a disaster. Time gives poetry to a battlefield, and perhaps Milly resembled a little the flower on an old rampart where an attack had been repulsed with heavy loss many years ago. Women passed him in the street marked on the forehead with ashes as though they had come up into the sunlight from underground. He remembered that it was Ash Wednesday.

In spite of the school-holiday Milly was not at home when he reached the house—perhaps she was still at Mass or perhaps she was away riding at the Country

Club. Lopez was demonstrating the Turbo Suction Cleaner
to a priest's housekeeper who had rejected the Atomic
Pile. Wormold's worst fears about the new model had
been justified, for he had not succeeded in selling a single
specimen. He went upstairs and opened the telegram; it
was addressed to a department at the British Consulate,
and the figures which followed had an ugly look like the
lottery tickets that remained unsold on the last day of a
draw. There was 2674 and then a string of five-figure
numerals. 42811 79145 72312 59200 80947 62533
10605 and so on. It was his first telegram and he noticed
that it was addressed from London. He was not even
certain (so long ago his lesson seemed) that he could
decode it, but he recognised a single group, 59200, which
had an abrupt and monitory appearance as though Hawthorne that moment had come accusingly up the stairs.
Gloomily he took down Lamb's *Tales from Shakespeare*—
how he had always detested Elia and the essay on Roast
Pork. The first group of figures, he remembered, indicated
the page, the line and the word with which the coding
began. "Dionysia, the wicked wife of Cleon," he read,
"met with an end proportionable to her deserts." He
began to decode from "deserts." To his surprise something
really did emerge. It was rather as though some strange
inherited parrot had begun to speak. "No. 1 of 24th
January following from 59200 begin paragraph A."

After working for three-quarters of an hour adding and
subtracting, he had decoded the whole message apart
from the final paragraph where something had gone
wrong either with himself or 59200, or perhaps with
Charles Lamb. "Following from 59200 begin paragraph
A nearly a month since membership Country Club approved and no repeat no information concerning proposed
sub-agents yet received stop trust you are not repeat not
recruiting any sub-agents before having them properly
traced stop begin paragraph B economic and political
report on lines of questionnaire left with you should be
despatched forthwith to 59200 stop begin paragraph C
cursed galloon must be forwarded kingston primary tuber-
cular message ends."

The last paragraph had an effect of angry incoherence which worried Wormold. For the first time it occurred to him that in their eyes—whoever *they* were—he had taken money and given nothing in return. This troubled him. It had seemed to him till then that he had been the recipient of an eccentric gift which had enabled Milly to ride at the Country Club and himself to order from England a few books he had coveted. The rest of the money was now on deposit in the bank; he half believed that some day he might be in a position to return it to Hawthorne.

He thought: I must do something, give them some names to trace, recruit an agent, keep them happy. He remembered how Milly used to play at shops and give him her pocket money for imaginary purchases. One had to play the child's game, but sooner or later Milly always required her money back.

He wondered how one recruited an agent. It was difficult for him to remember exactly how Hawthorne had recruited *him*—except that the whole affair had begun in a lavatory, but surely that was not an essential feature. He decided to begin with a reasonably easy case.

"You called me, Señor Vormell." For some reason the name Wormold was quite beyond Lopez' power of pronunciation, but as he seemed unable to settle on a satisfactory substitute, it was seldom that Wormold went by the same name twice.

"I want to talk to you, Lopez."

"*Si*, Señor Vomell."

Wormold said, "You've been with me a great many years now. We trust each other."

Lopez expressed the completeness of his trust with a gesture towards the heart.

"How would you like to earn a little more money each month?"

"Why, naturally . . . I was going to speak to you myself, Señor Ommel. I have a child coming. Perhaps twenty pesos?"

"This has nothing to do with the firm. Trade is too bad,

Lopez. This will be confidential work, for me personally, you understand."

"Ah yes, señor. Personal services I understand. You can trust me. I am discreet. Of course I will say nothing to the señorita."

"I think perhaps you *don't* understand."

"When a man reaches a certain age," Lopez said, "he no longer wishes to search for a woman himself, he wishes to rest from trouble. He wishes to command, 'Tonight yes, tomorrow night no.' To give his directions to someone he trusts . . ."

"I don't mean anything of the kind. What I was trying to say—well, it had nothing to do . . ."

"You do not need to be embarrassed in speaking to me, Señor Vormole. I have been with you many years."

"You are making a mistake," Wormold said. "I had no intention . . ."

"I understand that for an Englishman in your position places like the San Francisco are unsuitable. Even the Mamba Club."

Wormold knew that nothing he could say would check the eloquence of his assistant, now that he had embarked on the great Havana subject; the sexual exchange was not only the chief commerce of the city, but the whole *raison d'être* of a man's life. One sold sex or one bought it—immaterial which, but it was never given away.

"A youth needs variety," Lopez said, "but so too does a man of a certain age. For the youth it is the curiosity of ignorance, for the old it is the appetite which needs to be refreshed. No one can serve you better than I can, because I have studied you, Señor Venell. You are not a Cuban: for you the shape of a girl's bottom is less important than a certain gentleness of behaviour . . ."

"You have misunderstood me completely," Wormold said.

"The señorita this evening goes to a concert."

"How do you know?"

Lopez ignored the question. "While she is out, I will bring you a young lady to see. If you don't like her, I will bring another."

"You'll do nothing of the sort. Those are not the kind of services I want, Lopez. I want . . . well, I want you to keep your eyes and ears open and report to me . . ."

"On the señorita?"

"Good heavens no."

"Report on what then, Señor Vommold?"

Wormold said, "Well, things like . . ." But he hadn't the faintest idea on what subjects Lopez was capable of reporting. He remembered only a few points in the long questionnaire and none of them seemed suitable, "Possible Communist infiltration in the armed forces. Actual figures of sugar- and tobacco-production last year." Of course there were the contents of waste-paper baskets in the offices where Lopez serviced the cleaners, but surely even Hawthorne was joking when he spoke of the Dreyfus case—if those men ever joked.

"Like what, señor?"

Wormold said, "I'll let you know later. Go back to the shop now."

ii

It was the hour of the daiquiri, and in the Wonder Bar Dr. Hasselbacher was happy with his second Scotch. "You are worrying still, Mr. Wormold?" he said.

"Yes, I am worrying."

"Still the cleaner—the Atomic cleaner?"

"Not the cleaner." He drained his daiquiri and ordered another.

"Today you are drinking very fast."

"Hasselbacher, you've never felt the need of money, have you? But then, you have no child."

"Before long you will have no child either."

"I suppose not." The comfort was as cold as the daiquiri. "When the time comes, Hasselbacher, I want us both to be away from here. I don't want Milly woken up by any Captain Segura."

"That I can understand."

"The other day I was offered money."

"Yes?"

"To get information."

"What sort of information?"

"Secret information."

Dr. Hasselbacher sighed. He said, "You are a lucky man, Mr. Wormold. That information is always easy to give."

"Easy?"

"If it is secret enough, you alone know it. All you need is a little imagination, Mr. Wormold."

"They want me to recruit agents. How does one recruit an agent, Hasselbacher?"

"You could invent them too, Mr. Wormold."

"You sound as though you had experience."

"Medicine is my experience, Mr. Wormold. Have you never read the advertisement for secret remedies? A hair tonic confided by the dying Chief of a Red Indian tribe. With a secret remedy you don't have to print the formula. And there is something about a secret which makes people believe . . . perhaps a relic of magic. Have you read Sir James Frazer?"

"Have you heard of a book-code?"

"Don't tell me too much, Mr. Wormold, all the same. Secrecy is not my business—I have no child. Please don't invent me as your agent."

"No, I can't do that. These people don't like our friendship, Hasselbacher. They want me to stay away from you. They are tracing you. How do you suppose they trace a man?"

"I don't know. Be careful, Mr. Wormold. Take their money, but don't give them anything in return. You are vulnerable to the Seguras. Just lie and keep your freedom. They don't deserve truth."

"Whom do you mean by they?"

"Kingdoms, republic, powers." He drained his glass. "I must go and look at my culture, Mr. Wormold."

"Is anything happening yet?"

"Thank goodness, no. As long as nothing happens anything is possible, you agree? It is a pity that a lottery is ever drawn. I lose a hundred and forty thousand dollars a week, and I am a poor man."

"You won't forget Milly's birthday?"

"Perhaps the traces will be bad, and you will not want me to come. But remember, as long as you lie you do no harm."

"I take their money."

"They have no money except what they take from men like you and me."

He pushed open the half-door and was gone. Dr. Hasselbacher never talked in terms of morality; it was outside the province of a doctor.

iii

Wormold found a list of Country Club members in Milly's room. He knew where to look for it, between the latest volume of the *Horsewoman's Year Book* and a novel called *White Mare* by Miss "Pony" Traggers. He had joined the Country Club to find suitable agents, and here they all were in double column, over twenty pages of them. His eye caught an Anglo-Saxon name—Vincent C. Parkman; perhaps this was Earl's father. It seemed to Wormold that it was only right to keep the Parkmans in the family.

By the time he sat down to encode he had chosen two other names—an Engineer Cifuentes and a Professor Luis Sanchez. The professor, whoever he was, seemed a reasonable candidate for economic intelligence, the engineer could provide technical information, and Mr. Parkman, political. With the *Tales from Shakespeare* open before him (he had chosen for his key passage—"May that which follows be happy") he encoded "Number 1 of 25th January paragraph A begins I have recruited my assistant and assigned him the symbol 59200/5/1 stop proposed payment fifteen pesos a month stop paragraph B begins please trace the following. . . ."

All this paragraphing seemed to Wormold extravagant of time and money, but Hawthorne had told him it was part of the drill, just as Milly had insisted that all purchases from her shop should be wrapped in paper, even a single glass bead. "Paragraph C begins economic report as requested will follow shortly by bag."

There was nothing to do now but wait for the replies and to prepare the economic report. This troubled him. He had sent Lopez out to buy all the Government papers he could obtain on the sugar and tobacco industries—it was Lopez' first mission, and each day now he spent hours reading the local papers in order to mark any passage which could suitably be used by the professor or the engineer; it was unlikely that anyone in Kingston or London studied the daily papers of Havana. Even he found a new world in those badly printed pages; perhaps in the past he had depended too much on the *New York Times* or *Herald Tribune* for his picture of the world. Round the corner from the Wonder Bar a girl had been stabbed to death; "a martyr for love." Havana was full of martyrs of one kind or another. A man lost a fortune in one night at the Tropicana, climbed on the stage, embraced a coloured singer, then ran his car into the harbour and was drowned. Another man elaborately strangled himself with a pair of braces. There were miracles too; a virgin wept salt tears and a candle lit before Our Lady of Guadalupe burnt inexplicably for one week, from a Friday to a Friday. From this picture of violence and passion and love the victims of Captain Segura were alone excluded— they suffered and died without benefit of Press.

The economic report proved to be a tedious chore, for Wormold had never learnt to type with more than two fingers or to use the tabulator on his machine. It was necessary to alter the official statistics in case someone in the head office thought to compare the two reports, and sometimes Wormold forgot he had altered a figure. Addition and subtraction were never his strong points. A decimal point got shifted and had to be chased up and down a dozen columns. It was rather like steering a miniature car in a slot machine.

After a week he began to worry about the absence of replies. Had Hawthorne smelt a rat? But he was temporarily encouraged by a summons to the Consulate, where the sour clerk handed him a sealed envelope addressed for no reason he could understand to "Mr. Luke Penny." Inside the outer envelope was another envelope marked "Henry Leadbetter. Civilian Research Services"; a third envelope was inscribed 59200/5 and contained three months' wages and expenses in Cuban notes. He took them to the bank in Obispo.

"Office account, Mr. Wormold?"

"No. Personal." But he had a sense of guilt as the teller counted; he felt as though he had embezzled the company's money.

[2]

i

Ten days passed and no word reached him. He couldn't even send his economic report until the notional agent who supplied it had been traced and approved. The time arrived for his annual visit to retailers outside Havana, at Matanzas, Cienfuegos, Santa Clara and Santiago. Those towns he was in the habit of visiting by road in his ancient Hillman. Before leaving he sent a cable to Hawthorne. "On pretext of visiting sub-agents for vacuums propose to investigate possibilities for recruitment port of Matanzas, industrial centre Santa Clara, naval headquarters Cienfuegos and dissident centre Santiago calculate expenses of journey fifty dollars a day." He kissed Milly, made her promise to take no lifts in his absence from Captain Segura, and rattled off for a stirrup-cup in the Wonder Bar with Dr. Hasselbacher.

ii

Once a year, and always on his tour, Wormold wrote to his younger sister who lived in Northampton. (Perhaps writing to Mary momentarily healed the loneliness he felt at being away from Milly.) Invariably too he included the latest Cuban postage stamps for his nephew. The boy had begun to collect at the age of six and somehow, with the quick jog-trot of time, it slipped Wormold's memory that his nephew was now long past seventeen and had probably given up his collection years ago. In any case he must have been too old for the kind of note Wormold folded around the stamps; it was too juvenile even for Milly, and his nephew was her senior by several years.

"Dear Mark," Wormold wrote, "here are some stamps for your collection. It must be quite a big collection by now. I'm afraid these ones are not very interesting. I wish we had birds or beasts or butterflies in Cuba like the nice ones you showed me from Guatemala. Your affectionate uncle. P.S. I am sitting looking at the sea and it is very hot."

To his sister he wrote more explicitly, "I am sitting by the bay in Cienfuegos and the temperature is over ninety, though the sun has been down for an hour. They are showing Marilyn Monroe at the cinema, and there is one boat in the harbour called, oddly enough, the *Juan Belmonte*. (Do you remember that winter in Madrid when we went to the bullfight?) The Chief—I think he's the Chief—is sitting at the next table drinking Spanish brandy. There's nothing else for him to do except go to the cinema. This must be one of the quietest ports in the world. Just the pink and yellow street and a few cantinas and the big chimney of a sugar refinery and at the end of a weed-grown path the *Juan Belmonte*. Somehow I wish I could be sailing in it with Milly, but I don't know. Vacuum cleaners are not selling well—electric current is too uncertain in these troubled days. Last night at Matanzas the lights all went out three times—the first time I was in my bath. These are silly things to write all the way to Northampton.

"Don't think I am unhappy. There is a lot to be said for where we are. Sometimes I fear going home to Boots and Woolworths and cafeterias, and I'd be a stranger now even in the White Horse. The Chief has got a girl with him—I expect he has a girl in Matanzas too: he's pouring brandy down her throat as you give a cat medicine. The light here is wonderful just before the sun goes down: a long trickle of gold and the seabirds are dark patches on the pewter swell. The big white statue in the Paseo which looks in daylight like Queen Victoria is a lump of ectoplasm now. The bootblacks have all packed up their boxes under the arm-chairs in the pink colonnade: you sit high above the pavement as though on library-steps and rest your feet on the back of two little sea-horses in bronze that might have been brought here by a Phoenician. Why am I so nostalgic? I suppose because I have a little money tucked away and soon I must decide to go away for ever. I wonder if Milly will be able to settle down in a secretarial-training college in a grey street in north London.

"How is Aunt Alice and the famous wax in her ears? And how is Uncle Edward? or is he dead? I've reached the time of life when relatives die unnoticed."

He paid his bill and asked for the name of the Chief Engineer—it had struck him that he must have a few names checked when he got home, to justify his expenses.

iii

In Santa Clara his old Hillman lay down beneath him like a tired mule. Something was seriously wrong with its innards; only Milly would have known what. The man at the garage said that the repairs would take several days, and Wormold decided to go on to Santiago by coach. Perhaps in any case it was quicker and safer that way, for in the Oriente Province, where the usual rebels held the mountains and Government troops the roads and cities, blocks were frequent and buses were less liable to delay than private cars.

He arrived at Santiago in the evening, the empty dangerous hours of the unofficial curfew. All the shops in the piazza built against the Cathedral façade were closed. A single couple hurried across in front of the hotel; the night was hot and humid, and the greenery hung dark and heavy in the pallid light of half-strength lamps. In the reception office they greeted him with suspicion as though they assumed him to be a spy of one kind or another. He felt like an impostor, for this was a hotel of real spies, real police-informers and real rebel agents. A drunk man talked endlessly in the drab bar, as though he were saying in the style of Gertrude Stein "Cuba is Cuba is Cuba."

Wormold had for his dinner a dry flat omelette, stained and dog-eared like an old manuscript, and drank some sour wine. While he ate he wrote on a picture-postcard a few lines to Dr. Hasselbacher. Whenever he left Havana he despatched to Milly and Dr. Hasselbacher and sometimes even to Lopez bad pictures of bad hotels with a cross against one window like the cross in a detective story which indicates where the crime has been committed. "Car broken down. Everything very quiet. Hope to be back Thursday." A picture-postcard is a symptom of loneliness.

At nine o'clock Wormold set out to find his retailer. He had forgotten how abandoned the streets of Santiago were after dark. Shutters were closed behind the iron grills, and as in an occupied city the houses turned their backs on the passer-by. A cinema cast a little light, but no customer went in; by law it had to remain open, but no one except a soldier or a policeman was likely to visit it after dark. Down a side-street Wormold saw a military patrol go by.

Wormold sat with the retailer in a small hot room. An open door gave on to a patio, a palm tree and a well-head of wrought iron, but the air outside was as hot as the air within. They sat opposite each other in rocking-chairs, rocking towards each other and rocking away, making little currents of air.

Trade was bad—rock rock—nobody was busying electrical goods in Santiago—rock rock—what was the good? rock rock. As though to illustrate the point the electric light went out and they rocked in darkness.

Losing the rhythm their heads came into gentle collision.

"I'm sorry."

"My fault."

Rock rock rock.

Somebody scraped a chair in the patio.

"Your wife?" asked Wormold.

"No. Nobody at all. We are quite alone."

Wormold rocked forward, rocked back, rocked forward again, listening to the furtive movements in the patio.

"Of course." This was Santiago. Any house might contain a man on the run. It was best to hear nothing, and to see nothing was no problem, even when the light came half-heartedly back with a tiny yellow glow on the filament.

On his way to the hotel he was stopped by two policemen. They wanted to know what he was doing out so late..

"It's only ten o'clock," he said.

"What are you doing in this street at ten o'clock?"

"There's no curfew, is there?"

Suddenly, without warning, one of the policemen slapped his face. He felt shock rather than anger. He belonged to the law-abiding class; the police were his natural protectors. He put his hand to his cheek and said, "What in God's name do you think . . . ?" The other policeman with a blow in the back sent him stumbling along the pavement. His hat fell off into the filth of the gutter. He said, "Give me my hat," and felt himself pushed again. He began to say something about the British Consul and they swung him sideways across the road and sent him reeling. This time he landed inside a doorway in front of a desk where a man slept with his head on his arms. He woke up and shouted at Wormold—his mildest expression was "pig."

Wormold said, "I am a British subject, my name is Wormold, my address Havana—Lamparilla 37. My age forty-five, divorced, and I want to ring up the Consul."

The man who had called him a pig and who carried on his arm the chevron of a sergeant told him to show his passport.

"I can't. It's in my brief-case at the hotel."

One of his captors said with satisfaction, "Found on the street without papers."

"Empty his pockets," the sergeant said. They took out

his wallet and the picture-postcard to Dr. Hasselbacher, which he had forgotten to post, and a miniature whisky bottle, Old Granddad, that he had bought in the hotel-bar. The sergeant studied the bottle and the postcard.

He said, "Why do you carry this bottle? What does it contain?"

"What do you suppose?"

"The rebels make grenades out of bottles."

"Surely not such small bottles." The sergeant drew the cork, sniffed and poured a little on the palm of his hand. "It appears to be whisky," he said and turned to the postcard. He said, "Why have you made a cross on this picture?"

"It's the window of my room."

"Why show the window of your room?"

"Why shouldn't I? It's just—well, it's one of the things one does when travelling."

"Were you expecting a visitor by the window?"

"Of course not."

"Who is Dr. Hasselbacher?"

"An old friend."

"Is he coming to Santiago?"

"No."

"Then why do you want to show him where your room is?"

He began to realise what the criminal class knows so well, the impossibility of explaining anything to a man with power.

He said flippantly, "Dr. Hasselbacher is a woman."

"A woman doctor!" The sergeant exclaimed with disapproval.

"A doctor of philosophy. A very beautiful woman." He made two curves in the air.

"And she is joining you in Santiago?"

"No, no. But you know how it is with a woman, Sergeant? They like to know where their man is sleeping."

"You are her lover?" The atmosphere had changed for the better. "That still does not explain your wandering about the streets at night."

"There's no law . . ."

"No law, but prudent people stay at home. Only mis-chief-makers go out."

"I couldn't sleep for thinking of Emma."

"Who is Emma?"

"Dr. Hasselbacher."

The sergeant said slowly, "There is something wrong here. I can smell it. You are not telling me the truth. If you are in love with Emma, why are you in Santiago?"

"Her husband suspects."

"She has a husband? *No es muy agradable.* are you a Catholic?"

"No."

The sergeant picked up the postcard and studied it again. "The cross at a bedroom window—that is not very nice, either. How will she explain that to her husband?"

Wormold thought rapidly. "Her husband is blind."

"And that too is not nice. Not nice at all."

"Shall I hit him again?" one of the policemen asked.

"There is no hurry. I must interrogate him first. How long have you known this woman, Emma Hassel-bacher?"

"A week."

"A week? Nothing that you say is nice. You are a Protestant and an adulterer. When did you meet this woman?"

"I was introduced by Captain Segura."

The sergeant held the postcard suspended in mid-air. Wormold heard one of the policemen behind him swal-low. Nobody said anything for a long while.

"Captain Segura?"

"Yes."

"You know Captain Segura?"

"He is a friend of my daughter."

"So you have a daughter. You are married." He began to say again, "That is not n . . ." when one of the policemen interrupted him, "He knows Captain Se-gura."

"How can I tell that you are speaking the truth?"

"You could telephone to him and find out."

"It would take several hours to reach Havana on the telephone."

"I can't leave Santiago at night. I will wait for you at the hotel."

"Or in a cell at the station here."

"I don't think Captain Segura would be pleased."

The sergeant considered the matter for a long time, going through the contents of the wallet while he thought. Then he told one of the men to accompany Wormold back to the hotel and there to examine his passport (in this way the sergeant obviously thought that he was saving face). The two walked back in an embarrassed silence, and it was only when Wormold had lain down that he remembered the postcard to Dr. Hasselbacher was still on the sergeant's desk. It seemed to him to have no importance; he could always send another in the morning. How long it takes to realise in one's life the intricate patterns of which everything—even a picture-postcard—can form a part, and the rashness of dismissing anything as unimportant. Three days later Wormold took the bus back to Santa Clara; his Hillman was ready; the road to Havana offered him no problems.

[3]

A great many telegrams were waiting for him when he arrived in Havana in the late afternoon. There was also a note from Milly. "What have you been up to? You-know-who" (but he didn't) "very pressing—not in any bad way. Dr. Hasselbacher wants to speak to you urgently. Love. P.S. Riding at Country Club. Seraphina's picture taken by press photographer. Is this fame? Go, bid the soldiers shoot."

Dr. Hasselbacher could wait. Two of the telegrams were marked urgent.

"No. 2 of March 5 paragraph A begins trace of Hassel-

bacher ambiguous stop use utmost caution in any contact
and keep these to minimum message ends."

Vincent C. Parkman was rejected as an agent out of
hand. "You are not repeat not to contact him stop proba-
bility that he is already employed by American service."

The next telegram—No. 1 of March 4—read coldly,
"Please in future as instructed confine each telegram to
one subject."

No. 1 of March 5 was more encouraging, "No traces
Profesor Sanchez and Engineer Cifuentes stop you may
recruit them stop presumably men of their standing will
require no more than out-of-pocket expenses."

The last telegram was rather an anti-climax. "Following
from A.O. recruitment of 59200/5/1"—that was Lopez—
"recorded but please note proposed payment below recognised European scale and you should revise to 25 repeat 25
pesos monthly message ends."

Lopez was shouting up the stairs, "It is Dr. Hasselbacher."

"Tell him I'm busy. I'll call him later."

"He says will you come quick. He sounds strange."

Wormold went down to the telephone. Before he could
speak he heard an agitated and an old voice. It had never
occurred to him before that Dr. Hasselbacher was old.
"Please, Mr. Wormold . . ."

"Yes. What is it?"

"Please come to me. Something has happened."

"Where are you?"

"In my apartment."

"What's wrong, Hasselbacher?"

"I can't tell you over the telephone."

"Are you sick . . . hurt?"

"If only that were all," Hasselbacher said. "Please
come." In all the years they had known each other,
Wormold had never visited Hasselbacher's home. They
had met at the Wonder Bar, and on Milly's birthdays in a
restaurant, and once Dr. Hasselbacher had visited him in
Lamparilla when he had a high fever. There had been an
occasion too when he had wept in front of Hasselbacher,

sitting on a seat in the Paseo telling him that Milly's
mother had flown away on the morning plane to Miami,
but their friendship was safely founded on distance—it
was always the closest friendships that were most liable to
break. Now he even had to ask Hasselbacher how to find
his home.

"You don't know?" Hasselbacher asked in bewilderment.

"No."

"Please come quickly," Hasselbacher said, "I do not
wish to be alone."

But speed was impossible at this evening hour. Obispo
was a solid block of traffic, and it was half an hour before
Wormold reached the undistinguished block in which
Hasselbacher lived, twelve storeys high of livid stone.
Twenty years ago it had been modern, but the new steel
architecture to the West outsoared and outshone it. It
belonged to the age of tubular chairs, and a tubular chair
was what Wormold saw first when Dr. Hasselbacher let
him in. That and an old colour print of some castle on the
Rhine.

Dr. Hasselbacher like his voice had grown suddenly
old. It was not a question of colour. That seamed and
sanguine skin could change no more than a tortoise's and
nothing could bleach his hair whiter than the years had
already done. It was the expression which had altered. A
whole mood of life had suffered violence: Dr. Hasselbacher was no longer an optimist. He said humbly, "It is
good of you to come, Mr. Wormold." Wormold remembered the day when the old man had led him away from
the Paseo and filled him with drink in the Wonder Bar,
talking all the time, cauterising the pain with alcohol and
laughter and irresistible hope. He asked, "What has happened, Hasselbacher?"

"Come inside," Hasselbacher said.

The sitting-room was in confusion; it was as though a
malevolent child had been at work among the tubular
chairs, opening this, upsetting that, smashing and sparring
at the dictate of some irrational impulse. A photograph of
a group of young men holding beer mugs had been taken

from the frame and torn apart; a coloured reproduction of the Laughing Cavalier hung still on the wall over the sofa where one cushion out of three had been ripped open. The contents of a cupboard—old letters and bills—were scattered over the floor and a strand of very fair hair tied with black ribbon lay with a washed-up fish among the débris.

"Why?" Wormold asked.

"This does not matter so much," Hasselbacher said, "but come here."

A small room, which had been converted into a laboratory, was now reconverted into chaos. A gas-jet burnt yet among the ruins. Dr. Hasselbacher turned it off. He held up a test tube; the contents were smeared over the sink. He said, "You won't understand. I was trying to make a culture from—never mind. I knew nothing would come of it. It was a dream only." He sat heavily down on a tall tubular adjustable chair, which shortened suddenly under his weight and spilt him on the floor. Somebody always leaves a banana-skin on the scene of a tragedy. Hasselbacher got up and dusted his trousers.

"When did it happen?"

"Somebody telephoned to me—a sick call. I felt there was something wrong, but I had to go. I could not risk not going. When I came back there was *this*."

"Who did it?"

"I don't know. A week ago somebody called on me. A stranger. He wanted me to help him. It was not a doctor's job. I said no. He asked me whether my sympathies were with the East or the West. I tried to joke with him. I said they were in the middle." Dr. Hasselbacher said accusingly, "Once a few weeks ago you asked me the same question."

"I was only joking, Hasselbacher."

"I know. Forgive me. The worst thing they do is making all this suspicion." He stared into the sink. "An infantile dream. Of course I know that. Fleming discovered penicillin by an inspired accident. But an accident has to be inspired. An old second-rate doctor would never have an accident like that, but it was no business of theirs—was it?—if I wanted to dream."

"I don't understand. What's behind it? Something political? What nationality was this man?"

"He spoke English like I do, with an accent. Nowadays, all the world over, people speak with accents."

"Have you rung up the police?"

"For all I know," Dr. Hasselbacher said, "he *was* the police."

"Have they taken anything?"

"Yes. Some papers."

"Important?"

"I should never have kept them. They were more than thirty years old. When one is young one gets involved. No one's life is quite clean, Mr. Wormold. But I thought the past was the past. I was too optimistic. You and I are not like the people here—we have no confessional box where we can bury the bad past."

"You must have some idea . . . What will they do next?"

"Put me on a card-index perhaps," Dr. Hasselbacher said. "They have to make themselves important. Perhaps on the card I will be promoted to atomic scientist."

"Can't you start your experiment again?"

"Oh yes. Yes, I suppose so. But, you see, I never believed in it and now it has gone down the drain." He let a tap run to clear the sink. "I would only remember all this—dirt. That was a dream, this is reality." Something that looked like a fragment of toadstool stuck in the exit-pipe. He poked it down with his finger. "Thank you for coming, Mr. Wormold. You are a real friend."

"There is so little I can do."

"You let me talk. I am better already. Only I have this fear because of the papers. Perhaps it was an accident that they have gone. Perhaps I have overlooked them in all this mess."

"Let me help you search."

"No, Mr. Wormold. I wouldn't want you to see something of which I am ashamed."

They had two drinks together in the ruins of the sitting-room and then Wormold left. Dr. Hasselbacher was on his knees under the Laughing Cavalier, sweeping below the sofa. Shut in the car Wormold felt guilt nibbling around him like a mouse in a prison-cell. Perhaps soon the two of them would grow accustomed to each other and guilt would come to eat out of his hand. People similar to himself had done this, men who allowed themselves to be recruited while sitting in lavatories, who opened hotel doors with other men's keys and received instructions in secret ink and in novel uses for Lamb's *Tales from Shakespeare*. There was always another side to a joke, the side of the victim.

The bells were ringing in Santo Christo, and the doves rose from the roof in the golden evening and circled away over the lottery shops of O'Reilley Street and the banks of Obispo; little boys and girls, almost as indistinguishable in sex as birds streamed out from the School of the Holy Innocents in their black and white uniforms, carrying their little black satchels. Their age divided them from the adult world of 59200 and their credulity was of a different quality. He thought with tenderness, Milly will be home soon. He was glad that she could still accept fairy stories: a virgin who bore a child, pictures that wept or spoke words of love in the dark. Hawthorne and his kind were equally credulous, but what they swallowed were nightmares, grotesque stories out of science fiction.

What was the good of playing a game with half a heart? At least let him give them something they would enjoy for their money, something to put on their files better than an economic report. He wrote a rapid draft, "Number 1 of March 8 paragraph A begins in my recent trip to Santiago I heard reports from several sources of big military installations under construction in mountains of Oriente Province stop these constructions too extensive to be aimed at small rebel bands holding out there stop stories of widespread forest clearance under cover of forest fires stop peasants from several villages impressed to carry loads of stone paragraph B begins in bar of Santiago hotel met Spanish pilot of Cubana air line in advanced stage drunkenness stop he spoke of observing on flight

Havana–Santiago large concrete platforms too extensive
for any building paragraph C 59200/5/3 who accompa-
nied me to Santiago undertook dangerous mission near
military H.Q. at Bayamo and made drawings of strange
machinery in transport to forest stop these drawings will
follow by bag paragraph D have I your permission to pay
him bonus in view of serious risks of his mission and to
suspend work for a time on economic report in view
disquieting and vital nature of these reports from Oriente
paragraph E have you any traces Raul Dominguez Cubana pilot whom I propose to recruit as 59200/5/4."

Wormold joyfully encoded. He thought, I never believed I had it in me. He thought with pride, 59200/5
knows his job. His good humour even embraced Charles
Lamb. He chose for his passage page 217, line 12: "But I
will draw the curtain and show the picture. Is it not well
done?"

Wormold called Lopez from the shop. He handed him
twenty-five pesos. He said, "This is your first month's pay
in advance." He knew Lopez too well to expect any
gratitude for the extra five pesos, but all the same he was
a little taken aback when Lopez said, "Thirty pesos would
be a living wage."

"What do you mean, a living wage? The agency pays
you very well as it is."

"This will mean a great deal of work," Lopez said.

"It will, will it? What work?"

"Personal service."

"What personal service?"

"It must obviously be a great deal of work or you
wouldn't pay me twenty-five pesos." He had never been
able to get the better of Lopez in a financial argument.

"I want you to bring me an Atomic Pile from the
shop," Wormold said.

"We have only one in the store."

"I want it up here."

Lopez sighed. "Is that a personal service?"

"Yes."

When he was alone Wormold unscrewed the cleaner
into its various parts. Then he sat down at his desk and

began to make a series of careful drawings. As he sat back and contemplated his sketches of the sprayer detached from the hose-handle of the cleaner, the needle-jet, the nozzle and the telescopic tube, he wondered: Am I perhaps going too far? He realised that he had forgotten to indicate the scale. He ruled a line and numbered it off: one inch representing three feet. Then for better measure he drew a little man two inches high below the nozzle. He dressed him neatly in a dark suit, and gave him a bowler hat and an umbrella.

When Milly came home that evening he was still busy, writing his first report with a large map of Cuba spread over his desk.

"What are you doing, Father?"

"I am taking the first step in a new career."

She looked over his shoulder. "Are you becoming a writer?"

"Yes, an imaginative writer."

"Will that earn you a lot of money?"

"A moderate income, Milly, if I set my mind to it and write regularly. I plan to compose an essay like this every Saturday evening."

"Will you be famous?"

"I doubt it. Unlike most writers I shall give all the credit to my ghosts."

"Ghosts?"

"That's what they call those who do the real work while the author takes the pay. In my case I shall do the real work and it will be the ghosts who take the credit."

"But you'll have the pay?"

"Oh yes."

"Then can I buy a pair of spurs?"

"Certainly."

"Are you feeling all right, Father?"

"I never felt better. What a great sense of release you must have experienced when you set fire to Thomas Earl Parkman, Junior."

"Why do you go on bringing that up, Father? It was years ago."

"Because I admire you for it. Can't you do it again?"

"Of course not. I'm too old. Besides, there are no boys in the senior school. Father, one other thing. Could I buy a hunting flask?"

"Anything you like. Oh, wait. What are you going to put in it?"

"Lemonade."

"Be a good girl and fetch me a new sheet of paper. Engineer Cifuentes is a man of many words."

Interlude in London

"Had a good flight?" the Chief asked.

"A bit bumpy over the Azores," Hawthorne said. On this occasion he had not had time to change from his pale grey tropical suit; the summons had come to him urgently in Kingston and a car had met him at London Airport. He sat as close to the steam radiator as he could, but sometimes he couldn't help a shiver.

"What's that odd flower you're wearing?"

Hawthorne had quite forgotten it. He put his hand up to his lapel.

"It looks as though it had once been an orchid," the Chief said with disapproval.

"Pan American gave it us with our dinner last night," Hawthorne explained. He took out the limp mauve rag and put it in the ash-tray.

"With your dinner? What an odd thing to do," the Chief said. "It can hardly have improved the meal. Personally I detest orchids. Decadent things. There was someone, wasn't there, who wore green ones?"

"I only put it in my button-hole so as to clear the dinner-tray. There was so little room what with the hot cakes and champagne and the sweet salad and the tomato soup and the chicken Maryland and ice-cream . . ."

"What a terrible mixture. You should travel B.O.A.C."

"You didn't give me enough time, sir, to get a booking."

"Well, the matter is rather urgent. You know our man in Havana has been turning out some pretty disquieting stuff lately."

"He's a good man," Hawthorne said.

"I don't deny it. I wish we had more like him. What I can't understand is how the Americans have not tumbled to anything there."

"Have you asked them, sir?"

"Of course not. I don't trust their discretion."

"Perhaps they don't trust ours."

The Chief said, "Those drawings—did you examine them?"

"I'm not very knowledgeable that way, sir. I sent them straight on."

"Well, take a good look at them now."

The Chief spread the drawings over his desk. Hawthorne reluctantly left the radiator and was immediately shaken by a shiver.

"Anything the matter?"

"The temperature was ninety-two yesterday in Kingston."

"Your blood's getting thin. A spell of cold will do you good. What do you think of them?"

Hawthorne stared at the drawings. They reminded him of—something. He was touched, he didn't know why, by an odd uneasiness.

"You remember the reports that came with them," the Chief said. "The source was stroke three. Who is he?"

"I think that would be Engineer Cifuentes, sir."

"Well, even he was mystified. With all his technical knowledge. These machines were being transported by lorry from the army-headquarters at Bayamo to the edge of the forest. Then mules took over. General direction those unexplained concrete platforms."

"What does the Air Ministry say, sir?"

"They are worried, very worried. Interested too, of course."

"What about the atomic research people?"

"We haven't shown them the drawings yet. You know what those fellows are like. They'll criticise points of detail, say the whole thing is unreliable, that the tube is out of proportion or points the wrong way. You can't expect an agent working from memory to get every detail right. I want photographs, Hawthorne."

"That's asking a lot, sir."

"We have got to have them. At any risk. Do you know what Savage said to me? I can tell you, it gave me a very nasty nightmare. He said that one of the drawings reminded him of a giant vacuum cleaner."

"A vacuum cleaner!" Hawthorne bent down and examined the drawings again, and the cold struck him once more.

"Makes you shiver, doesn't it?"

"But that's impossible, sir." He felt as though he were pleading for his own career, "It couldn't be a vacuum cleaner, sir. Not a vacuum cleaner."

"Fiendish, isn't it?" the Chief said. "The ingenuity, the simplicity, the devilish imagination of the thing." He removed his black monocle and his baby-blue eye caught the light and made it jig on the wall over the radiator. "See this one here six times the height of a man. Like a gigantic spray. And this—what does this remind you of?"

Hawthorne said unhappily, "A two-way nozzle."

"What's a two-way nozzle?"

"You sometimes find them with a vacuum cleaner."

"Vacuum cleaner again. Hawthorne, I believe we may be on to something so big that the H-bomb will become a conventional weapon."

"Is that desirable, sir?"

"Of course it's desirable. Nobody worries about conventional weapons."

"What have you in mind, sir?"

"I'm no scientist," the Chief said, "but look at this great tank. It must stand nearly as high as the forest-trees. A huge gaping mouth at the top, and this pipe-line—the man's only indicated it. For all we know, it may extend for miles—from the mountains to the sea perhaps. You know the Russians are said to be working on some idea—something to do with the power of the sun, sea-evaporation. I don't know what it's all about, but I do know this thing is Big. Tell our man we must have photographs."

"I don't quite see how he can get near enough . . ."

"Let him charter a plane and lose his way over the area. Not himself personally, of course, but stroke three or stroke two. Who is stroke two?"

"Professor Sanchez, sir. But he'd be shot down. They have air-force planes patrolling all that section."

"They have, have they?"

"To spot for rebels."

"So they say. Do you know, I've got a hunch, Hawthorne."

"Yes, sir?"

"That the rebels don't exist. They're purely notional. It gives the Government all the excuse it needs to shut down a censorship over the area."

"I hope you are right, sir."

"It would be better for all of us," the Chief said with exhilaration, "if I were wrong. I fear these things, I fear them, Hawthorne." He put back his monocle and the light left the wall. "Hawthorne, when you were here last did you speak to Miss Jenkinson about a secretary for 59200 stroke 5?"

"Yes, sir. She had no obvious candidate, but she thought a girl called Beatrice would do."

"Beatrice? How I hate all these Christian names. Fully trained?"

"Yes."

"The time has come to give our man in Havana some help. This is altogether too big for an untrained agent with no assistance. Better send a radio-operator with her."

"Wouldn't it be a good thing if I went over first and saw him? I could take a look at things and have a talk with him."

"Bad security, Hawthorne. We can't risk blowing him now. With a radio he can communicate direct with London. I don't like this tie-up with the Consulate, nor do they."

"What about his reports, sir?"

"He'll have to organise some kind of courier-service to Kingston. One of his travelling salesmen. Send out instructions with the secretary. Have you seen her?"

"No, sir."

"See her at once. Make sure she's the right type. Capable of taking charge on the technical side. You'll have to put her *au fait* with his establishment. His old secretary will have to go, Speak to the A.O. about a reasonable pension until her natural date for retirement."

"Yes, sir," Hawthorne said. "Could I take one more look at those drawings?"

"That one seems to interest you What's your idea of it?"

"It looks," Hawthorne said miserably, "like a snap-action coupling."

When he was at the door the Chief spoke again. "You know, Hawthorne, we owe a great deal of this to you. I was told once that you were no judge of men, but I backed my private judgment. Well done, Hawthorne."

"Thank you, sir." He had his hand on the door-knob.

"Hawthorne."

"Yes, sir?"

"Did you find that penny note-book?"

"No, sir."

"Perhaps Beatrice will."

PART III

[1]

It was not a night Wormold was ever likely to forget. He had chosen on Milly's seventeenth birthday to take her to the Tropicana. It was a more innocent establishment than the Nacional in spite of the roulette-rooms, through which visitors passed before they reached the cabaret. Stage and dance-floor were open to the sky. Chorus-girls paraded twenty feet up along the great palm-trees, while pink and mauve searchlights swept the floor. A man in bright blue evening clothes sang in Anglo-American about Paree. Then the piano was wheeled away into the undergrowth, and the dancers stepped down like awkward birds from among the branches.

"It's like the Forest of Arden," Milly said ecstatically. The duenna wasn't there: she had left after the first glass of champagne.

"I don't think there were palms in the Forest of Arden. Or dancing girls."

"You are so literal, Father."

"You like Shakespeare?" Dr. Hasselbacher asked.

"Oh, not Shakespeare—there's far too much poetry. You know the kind of thing—Enter a messenger. 'My Lord the Duke advances on the right.' 'Thus make we with glad heart towards the fight.' "

"Is that Shakespeare?"

"It's like Shakespeare."

"What nonsense you talk, Milly."

"All the same the Forest of Arden is Shakespeare too, I think," Dr. Hasselbacher said.

"Yes, but I only read him in Lamb's *Tales from Shakespeare*. He cuts out all the messengers and the sub-Dukes and the poetry."

"They give you that at school?"

"Oh no, I found a copy in Father's room."

"You read Shakespeare in that form, Mr. Wormold?" Dr. Hasselbacher asked with some surprise.

"Oh no, no. Of course not. I really bought it for Milly."

"Then why were you so cross the other day when I borrowed it?"

"I wasn't cross. It was just that I don't like you poking about . . . among things that don't concern you."

"You talk as though I were a spy," Milly said.

"Dear Milly, please don't quarrel on your birthday. You are neglecting Dr. Hasselbacher."

"Why are you so silent, Dr. Hasselbacher?" Milly asked, pouring out her second glass of champagne.

"One day you must lend me Lamb's *Tales,* Milly. I too find Shakespeare difficult."

A very small man in a very tight uniform waved his hand towards their table.

"You aren't worried are you, Dr. Hasselbacher?"

"What should I be worried about, dear Milly, on your birthday? Except about the years of course."

"Is seventeen so old?"

"For me they have gone too quickly."

The man in the tight uniform stood by their table and bowed. His face had been pocked and eroded like the pillars on the sea-front. He carried a chair which was almost as big as himself.

"This is Captain Segura, Father."

"May I sit down?" He inserted himself between Milly and Dr. Hasselbacher without waiting for Wormold's reply. He said, "I am so glad to meet Milly's father." He had an easy rapid insolence you had no time to resent before he had given fresh cause for annoyance. "Introduce me to your friend, Milly."

"This is Dr. Hasselbacher."

Captain Segura ignored Dr. Hasselbacher and filled Milly's glass. He called a waiter. "Bring me another bottle."

"We are just going, Captain Segura," Wormold said.

"Nonsense. You are my guest. It is only just after midnight."

Wormold's sleeve caught a glass. It fell and smashed, like the birthday party. "Waiter, another glass." Segura began to sing softly, "The rose I plucked in the garden," leaning towards Milly, turning his back on Dr. Hassel-bacher.

Milly said, "You are behaving very badly."

"Badly? To you?"

"To all of us. This is my seventeenth birthday party, and it's my father's party—not yours."

"Your seventeenth birthday? Then you must certainly be my guests. I'll invite some of the dancers to our ta-ble."

"We don't want any dancers," Milly said.|

"I am in disgrace?"

"Yes."

"Ah," he said with pleasure, "it was because today I was not outside the school to pick you up. But, Milly, sometimes I have to put police-work first. Waiter, tell the conductor to play 'Happy Birthday to You.' "

"Do no such thing," Milly said. "How can you be so—so vulgar?"

"Me? Vulgar?" Captain Segura laughed happily. "She is such a little jester," he said to Wormold. "I like to joke too. That is why we get on so well together."

"She tells me you have a cigarette-case made out of human skin."

"How she teases me about that. I tell her that her skin would make a lovely . . ."

Dr. Hasselbacher got up abruptly. He said, "I am going to watch the roulette."

"He doesn't like me?" Captain Segura asked. "Perhaps he is an old admirer, Milly? A very old admirer, ha ha!"

"He's an old friend," Wormold said.

"But you and I, Mr. Wormold, know that there is no such thing as friendship between a man and a woman."

"Milly is not yet a woman."

"You speak like a father, Mr. Wormold. No father knows his daughter."

Wormold looked at the champagne bottle and at Cap-tain Segura's head. He was sorely tempted to bring them together. At a table immediately behind the Captain, a young woman whom he had never seen before gave Wormold a grave encouraging nod. He touched the champagne bottle and she nodded again. She must, he thought, be as clever as she was pretty to have read his thoughts so accurately. He was envious of her companions, two pilots from K.L.M. and an air-hostess.

"Come and dance, Milly," Captain Segura said, "and show that I am forgiven."

"I don't want to dance."

"Tomorrow I swear I will be waiting at the convent-gates."

Wormold made a little gesture as much as to say, "I haven't the nerve. Help me." The girl watched him seriously; it seemed to him that she was considering the whole of the situation and any decision she reached would be final and call for immediate action. She siphoned some soda into her whisky.

"Come, Milly. You must not spoil my party."

"It's not your party. It's Father's."

"You stay angry so long. You must understand that sometimes I have to put work even before my dear little Milly."

The girl behind Captain Segura altered the angle of the siphon.

"No," Wormold said instinctively, "no." The spout of the siphon was aimed upwards at Captain Segura's neck. The girl's finger was ready for action. He was hurt that anyone so pretty should look at him with such contempt. He said, "Yes. Please. Yes," and she triggered the siphon. The stream of soda hissed off Captain Segura's neck and ran down the back of his collar. Dr. Hasselbacher's voice called "Bravo" from among the tables. Captain Segura exclaimed *"Coño."*

"I'm so sorry," the young woman said. "I meant it for my whisky."

"Your whisky!"

"Dimpled Haig," the girl said. Milly giggled.

Captain Segura bowed stiffly. You could not estimate his danger from his size any more than you could a hard drink.

Dr. Hasselbacher said, "You have finished your siphon, madam, let me find you another." The Dutchmen at the table whispered together uncomfortably.

"I don't think I'm to be trusted with another," the girl said.

Captain Segura squeezed out a smile. It seemed to come from the wrong place like toothpaste when the tube splits. He said, "For the first time I have been shot in the back. I am glad that it was by a woman." He had made an admirable recovery; the water still dripped from his hair and his collar was limp with it. He said, "Another time I would have offered you a return match, but I am late at the barracks. I hope I may see you again?"

"I am staying here," she said.

"On holiday?"

"No. Work."

"If you have any trouble with your permit," he said ambiguously, "you must come to me. Good night, Milly. Good night, Mr. Wormold. I will tell the waiter that you are my guests. Order what you wish."

"He made a creditable exit," the girl said.

"It was a creditable shot."

"To have hit him with a champagne bottle might have been a bit exaggerated. Who is he?"

"A lot of people call him the Red Vulture."

"He tortures prisoners," Milly said.

"I seem to have made quite a friend of him."

"I wouldn't be too sure of that," Dr. Hasselbacher said.

They joined their tables together. The two pilots bowed and gave unpronounceable names. Dr. Hasselbacher said with horror to the Dutchmen, "You are drinking Coca-Cola."

"It is the regulation. We take off at 3:30 for Montreal."

Wormold said, "If Captain Segura is going to pay, let's have more champagne. And Coca-Cola."

"I don't think I can drink any more Coca-Cola, can you, Hans?"

"I could drink a Bols," the younger pilot said.

"You can have no Bols," the air-hostess told him firmly, "before Amsterdam."

The young pilot whispered to Wormold, "I wish to marry her."

"Who?"

"Miss Pfunk," or so it sounded.

"Won't she?"

"No."

The elder Dutchman said, "I have a wife and three children." He unbuttoned his breast-pocket. "I have their photographs here."

He handed Wormold a coloured card showing a girl in a tight yellow sweater and bathing-drawers adjusting her skates. The sweater was marked Mamba Club, and below the picture Wormold read, "We guarantee you a lot of fun. Fifty beautiful girls. You won't be alone."

"I don't think this is the right picture," Wormold said.

The young woman, who had chestnut hair and, as far as he could tell in the confusing Tropicana lights, hazel eyes, said, "Let's dance."

"I'm not very good at dancing."

"It doesn't matter, does it?"

He shuffled her around. She said, "I see what you mean. This is meant to be a rumba. Is that your daughter?"

"Yes."

"She's very pretty."

"Have you just arrived?"

"Yes. The crew were making a night of it, so I joined up with them. I don't know anybody here." Her head reached his chin and he could smell her hair; it touched his mouth as they moved. He was vaguely disappointed that she wore a wedding-ring. She said, "My name's Severn. Beatrice Severn."

"Mine's Wormold."

"Then I'm your secretary," she said.

"What do you mean? I have no secretary."

"Oh yes you have. Didn't they tell you I was coming?"

"No." He didn't need to ask who "they" were.

"But I sent the telegram myself."

"There was one last week—but I couldn't make head or tail of it."

"What's your edition of Lamb's *Tales?*"

"Everyman."

"Damn. They gave me the wrong edition. I suppose the telegram *was* rather a mess. Anyway, I'm glad I found you."

"I'm glad too. A bit taken aback, of course. Where are you staying?"

"The Inglaterra tonight, and then I thought I'd move in."

"Move in where?"

"To your office, of course. I don't mind where I sleep. I'll just doss down in one of your staff-rooms."

"There aren't any. It's a very small office."

"Well, there's a secretary's room anyway."

"But I've never had a secretary, Mrs. Severn."

"Call me Beatrice. It's suppose to be good for security."

"Security?"

"It is rather a problem if there isn't even a secretary's room. Let's sit down."

A man, wearing a conventional black dinner jacket among the jungle trees like an English district officer was singing:

> Sane men surround
> You, old family friends.
> They say the earth is round—
> My madness offends.
> An orange has pips, they say,
> And an apple has rind.
> I say that night is day
> And I've no axe to grind.
>
> Please don't believe . . .

They sat at an empty table at the back of the roulette-room. They could hear the hiccup of the little balls. She wore her grave look again—a little self-consciously like a girl in her first long gown. She said, "If I had known I was your secretary I would never have siphoned that police-man—without your telling me."

"You don't have to worry."

"I was really sent here to make things easier for you. Not more difficult."

"Captain Segura doesn't matter."

"You see, I've had a very full training. I've passed in codes and microphotography. I can take over contact with your agents."

"Oh."

"You've done so well they're anxious you should take no risk of being blown. It doesn't matter so much if I'm blown."

"I'd hate to see you blown. Half-blown would be all right."

"I don't understand."

"I was thinking of roses."

She said, "Of course, as that telegram was mutilated, you don't even know about the radio-operator."

"I don't."

"He's at the Inglaterra too. Air-sick. We have to find room for him as well."

"If he's air-sick perhaps . . ."

"You can make him assistant accountant. He's been trained for that."

"But I don't need one. I haven't even got a chief accountant."

"Don't worry. I'll get things straight in the morning. That's what I'm here for."

"There's something about you," Wormold said, "that reminds me of my daughter. Do you say novenas?"

"What are they?"

"You don't know? Thank God for that."

The man in the dinner jacket was finishing his song.

I say that winter's May
And I've no axe to grind.

The lights changed from blue to rose and the dancers
went back to perch among the palm-trees. The dice rattled at the crap-tables, and Milly and Dr. Hasselbacher
made their way happily towards the dance-floor. It was as
though her birthday had been constructed again out of its
broken pieces.

[2]

i

Next morning Wormold was up early. He had a slight
hangover from the champagne, and the unreality of the
Tropicana night extended into the office-day. Beatrice
had told him he was doing well—she was the mouthpiece
of Hawthorne and "those people." He had a sense of
disappointment at the thought that she like Hawthorne
belonged to the national world of his agents. His
agents . . .

He sat down before his card-index. He had to make his
cards look as plausible as possible before she came. Some of
the agents seemed to him now to verge on the improba-
ble. Professor Sanchez and Engineer Cifuentes were
deeply committed, he couldn't get rid of them; they had
drawn nearly two hundred pesos in expenses. Lopez was
a fixture too. The drunken pilot of the Cubana air line
had received a handsome bonus of five hundred pesos for
the story of the construction in the mountains, but perhaps
he could be jettisoned as insecure. There was the Chief
Engineer of the *Juan Belmonte* whom he had seen drinking in Cienfuegos—he seemed a character probable
enough and he was only drawing seventy-five pesos a
month. But there were other characters whom he feared
might not bear close inspection: Rodriguez, for example,

described on his card as a night-club king, and Teresa, a dancer at the Shanghai Theatre whom he had listed as the mistress simultaneously of the Minister of Defence and the Director of Posts and Telegraphs (it was not surprising that London had found no trace of either Rodriguez or Teresa). He was ready to jettison Rodriguez, for anyone who came to know Havana well would certainly question his existence sooner or later. But he could not bear to relinquish Teresa. She was his only woman spy, his Mata Hari. It was unlikely that his new secretary would visit the Shanghai, where three pornographic films were shown nightly between nude dances.

Milly sat down beside him. "What are all these cards?" she asked.

"Customers."

"Who was that girl last night?"

"She's going to be my secretary."

"How grand you are getting."

"Do you like her?"

"I don't know. You didn't give me a chance to talk to her. You were too busy dancing and spooning."

"I wasn't spooning."

"Does she want to marry you?"

"Good heavens, no."

"Do you want to marry her?"

"Milly, do be sensible. I only met her last night."

"Marie, a French girl at the convent, says that all true love is a *coup de foudre*."

"Is that the kind of thing you talk about at the convent?"

"Naturally. It's the future, isn't it? We haven't got a past to talk about, though Sister Agnes has."

"Who is Sister Agnes?"

"I've told you about her. She's the sad and lovely one. Marie says she had an unhappy *coup de foudre* when she was young."

"Did she tell Marie that?"

"No, of course not. But Marie knows. She's had two unhappy *coups de foudre* herself. They came quite suddenly, out of a clear sky."

"I'm old enough to be safe."

"Oh no. There was an old man—he was nearly fifty—who had a *coup de foudre* for Marie's mother. He was married, like you."

"Well, my secretary's married too, so that should be all right."

"Is she really married or a lovely widow?"

"I don't know. I haven't asked her. Do you think she's lovely?"

"Rather lovely. In a way."

Lopez called up the stairs, "There is a lady here. She says you expect her."

"Tell her to come up."

"I'm going to stay," Milly warned him.

"Beatrice, this is Milly."

Her eyes, he noticed, were the same colour as the night before and so was her hair; it had not after all been the effect of the champagne and the palm-trees. He thought, She looks real.

"Good morning. I hope you had a good night," Milly said in the voice of the duenna.

"I had terrible dreams." She looked at Wormold and the card-index and Milly. She said, "I enjoyed last night."

"You were wonderful with the soda-water siphon," Milly said generously, "Miss . . ."

"Mrs. Severn. But please call me Beatrice."

"Oh, are you married?" Milly asked with phony curiosity.

"I *was* married."

"Is he dead?"

"Not that I know of. He sort of faded away."

"Oh."

"It does happen with his type."

"What was his type?"

"Milly, it's time you were off. You've no business asking Mrs. Severn—Beatrice . . ."

"At my age," Milly said, "one has to learn from other people's experiences."

"You are quite right. I suppose you'd call his type

intellectual and sensitive. I thought he was very beautiful; he had a face like a young fledgling looking out of a nest in one of those nature films and fluff-like feathers round his Adam's apple, a rather large Adam's apple. The trouble was when he got to forty he still looked like a fledgling. Girls loved him. He used to go to UNESCO conferences in Venice and Vienna and places like that. Have you a safe, Mr. Wormold?"

"No."

"What happened?" Milly asked.

"Oh, I got to see through him. I mean literally, not in a nasty way. He was very thin and concave and he got sort of transparent. When I looked at him I could see all the delegates sitting there between his ribs and the chief speaker rising and saying, 'Freedom is of importance to creative writers.' It was very uncanny at breakfast."

"And don't you know if he's alive?"

"He was alive last year, because I saw in the papers that he read a paper on 'The Intellectual and the Hydrogen Bomb' at Taormina. You ought to have a safe, Mr. Wormold."

"Why?"

"You can't leave things just lying about. Besides, it's expected of an old-fashioned merchant-king like you."

"Who called me an old-fashioned merchant-king?"

"It's the impression they have in London. I'll go out and find you a safe right away."

"I'll be off," Milly said. "You'll be sensible, won't you, Father? You know what I mean."

ii

It proved to be an exhausting day. First Beatrice went out and procured a large combination-safe, which required a lorry and six men to transport it. They broke the banisters and a picture while getting it up the stairs. A crowd collected outside, including several truants from the school next door, two beautiful negresses and a policeman. When Wormold complained that the affair was making him conspicuous, Beatrice reported that the way to become really conspicuous was to try to escape notice.

"For example, that siphon," she said. "Everybody will remember me as the woman who siphoned the policeman. Nobody will ask questions any more about who I am. They have the answer."

While they were still struggling with the safe a taxi drove up and a young man got out and unloaded the largest suitcase Wormold had ever seen. "This is Rudy," Beatrice said.

"Who is Rudy?"

"Your assistant accountant. I told you last night."

"Thank God," Wormold said, "there seems to be something I've forgotten about last night."

"Come along in, Rudy, and relax."

"It's no earthly use telling him to come in," Wormold said. "Come in where? There's no room for him."

"He can sleep in the office," Beatrice said.

"There isn't enough room for a bed and that safe and my desk."

"I'll get you a smaller desk. How's the air-sickness, Rudy? This is Mr. Wormold, the boss."

Rudy was very young and very pale and his fingers were stained yellow with nicotine or acid. He said, "I vomited twice in the night, Beatrice. They've broken a Röntgen tube."

"Never mind that now. We'll just get the preliminaries fixed. Go off and buy a camp-bed."

"Righto," Rudy said and disappeared. One of the negresses sidled up to Beatrice and said, "I'm British."

"So am I," Beatrice said, "glad to meet you."

"You the gel who poured water on Captain Segura?"

"Well, more or less. Actually I squirted."

The negress turned and explained to the crowd in Spanish. Several people clapped. The policeman moved away, looking embarrassed. The negress said, "You very lovely gel, miss."

"You're pretty lovely yourself," Beatrice said. "Give me a hand with this case." They struggled with Rudy's suitcase, pushing and pulling.

"Excuse me," a man said, elbowing through the crowd, "excuse me, please."

"What do you want?" Beatrice asked. "Can't you see we are busy? Make an appointment."

"I only want to buy a vacuum cleaner."

"Oh, a vacuum cleaner. I suppose you'd better go inside. Can you climb over the suitcase?"

Wormold called to Lopez, "Look after him. For goodness' sake, try and sell him an Atomic Pile. We haven't sold one yet."

"Are you going to live here?" the negress asked.

"I'm going to work here. Thanks a lot for your help."

"We Britishers have to stick together," the negress said.

The men who had been setting up the safe came downstairs spitting on their hands and rubbing them on their jeans to show how hard it had all been. Wormold tipped them. He went upstairs and looked gloomily at his office. The chief trouble was that there was just room for a camp-bed, which robbed him of any excuse. He said, "There's nowhere for Rudy to keep his clothes."

"Rudy's used to roughing it. Anyway there's your desk. You can empty what's in the drawers into your safe and Rudy can keep his things in them."

"I've never used a combination."

"It's perfectly simple. You choose three sets of numbers you can keep in your head. What's your street-number?"

"I don't know."

"Well, your telephone-number—no, that's not secure. It's the kind of thing a burglar might try. What's the date of your birth?"

"1914."

"And your birthday?"

"6th December."

"Well then, let's make it 19-6-14."

"I won't remember that."

"Oh yes, you will. You can't forget your own birthday. Now watch me. You turn the knob anti-clockwise four times, then forward to 19, clockwise three times, then to

6, anti-clockwise twice, forward to 14, whirl it round and it's locked. Now you unlock it the same way—19-6-14 and hey presto, it opens." In the safe was a dead mouse. Beatrice said, "Shop-soiled, I should have got a reduction."

She began to open Rudy's case, pulling out bits and pieces of radio-set, batteries, camera-equipment, mysterious tubes wrapped up in Rudy's socks. Wormold said, "How on earth did you bring all that stuff through the customs?"

"We didn't. 59200 stroke 4 stroke 5 brought it for us from Kingston."

"Who's he?"

"A Creole smuggler. He smuggles in cocaine, opium and marijuana. Of course he has the customs all lined up. This time they assumed it was his usual cargo."

"It would need a lot of drugs to fill that case."

"Yes. We had to pay rather heavily."

She stowed everything quickly and neatly away after emptying his drawers into the safe. She said, "Rudy's shirts are going to get a bit crushed, but never mind."

"I don't."

"What are these?" she asked, picking up the cards he had been examining.

"My agents."

"You mean you keep them lying about on your desk?"

"Oh, I lock them away at night."

"You haven't got much idea of security, have you?" She looked at a card. "Who is Teresa?"

"She dances naked."

"Quite naked?"

"Yes."

"How interesting for you. London wants me to take over contact with your agents. Will you introduce me to Teresa some time when she's got her clothes on?"

Wormold said, "I don't think she'd work for a woman. You know how it is with these girls."

"I don't. You do. Ah, Engineer Cifuentes. London

thinks a lot of him. You can't say he would mind working for a woman."

"He doesn't speak English."

"Perhaps I could learn Spanish. That wouldn't be a bad cover, taking Spanish lessons. Is he as good-looking as Teresa?"

"He's got a very jealous wife."

"Oh, I think I could deal with her."

"It's absurd, of course, because of his age."

"What's his age?"

"Sixty-five. Besides, there's no other woman who would look at him because of his paunch. I'll ask him about the Spanish lessons if you like."

"No hurry. We'll leave it for the moment. I could start with this other one. Professor Sanchez. I got used to intellectuals with my husband."

"He doesn't speak English either."

"I expect he speaks French. My mother was French. I'm bi-lingual."

"I don't know whether he does or not. I'll find out."

"You know, you oughtn't to have all these names written like this *en clair* on the cards. Suppose Captain Segura investigated you. I'd hate to think of Engineer Cifuentes's paunch being skinned to make a cigarette-case. Just put enough details under their symbol to remember them by—59200 stroke 5 stroke 3—jealous wife and paunch. I will write them for you and burn the old ones. Damn. Where are those celluloid sheets?"

"Celluloid sheets?"

"To help burn papers in a hurry. Oh, I expect Rudy put them in his shirts."

"What a lot of knick-knacks you carry around."

"Now we've got to arrange the darkroom."

"I haven't got a darkroom."

"Nobody has nowadays. I've come prepared. Blackout curtains and a red globe. And a microscope, of course."

"What do we want a microscope for?"

"Microphotography. You see, if there's anything really urgent that you can't put in a telegram, London wants us to communicate direct and save all the time it takes via

Kingston. We can send a microphotograph in an ordinary letter. You stick it on as a full stop and they float the letter in water until the dot comes unstuck. I suppose you do write letters home sometimes. Business letters . . . ?"

"I send those to New York."

"Friends and relations?"

"I've lost touch in the last ten years. Except with my sister. Of course I send Christmas cards."

"We mightn't be able to wait till Christmas."

"Sometimes I send postage stamps to a small nephew."

"The very thing. We could put a microphotograph on the back of one of the stamps."

Rudy came heavily up the stairs carrying his camp-bed, and the picture-frame was broken all over again. Beatrice and Wormold retired into the next room to give him space and sat on Wormold's bed. There was a lot of banging and clanking and something broke.

"Rudy isn't very good with his hands," Beatrice said. Her gaze wandered. She said, "Not a single photograph. Have you no private life?"

"I don't think I have much. Except for Milly. And Dr. Hasselbacher.

"London doesn't like Dr. Hasselbacher."

"London can go to hell," Wormold said. He suddenly wanted to describe to her the ruin of Dr. Hasselbacher's flat and the destruction of his futile experiments. He said, "It's people like your folk in London . . . I'm sorry. You are one of them."

"So are you."

"Yes, of course. So am I."

Rudy called from the other room, "I've got it fixed."

"I wish you weren't one of them," Wormold said.

"It's a living," she said.

"It's not a real living. All this spying. Spying on what? Secret agents discovering what everybody knows already . . ."

"Or just making it up," she said. He stopped short, and she went on without a change of voice, "There are lots of other jobs that aren't real. Designing a new plastic soapbox, making pokerwork jokes for public-houses, writing advertising slogans, being an M.P., talking to UNESCO conferences. But the money's real. What happens after work is real. I mean, your daughter is real and her seventeenth birthday is real."

"What do you do after work?"

"Nothing much now, but when I was in love . . . we went to cinemas and drank coffee in Espresso bars and sat on summer evenings in the Park."

"What happened?"

"It takes two to keep something real. He was acting all the time. He thought he was the great lover. Sometimes I almost wished he would turn impotent for a while just so that he'd lose his confidence. You can't love and be as confident as he was. If you love you are afraid of losing it, aren't you?" She said, "Oh hell, why am I telling you all this? Let's go and make microphotographs and code some cables." She looked through the door. "Rudy's lying on his bed. I suppose he's feeling air-sick again. Can you be air-sick all this while? Haven't you got a room where there isn't a bed? Beds always make one talk." She opened another door. "Table laid for lunch. Cold meat and salad. Two places. Who does all this? A little fairy?"

"A woman comes in for two hours in the morning."

"And the room beyond?"

"That's Milly's. It's got a bed in it too."

[3]

i

The situation, whichever way he looked at it, was uncomfortable. Wormold was in the habit now of drawing occasional expenses for Engineer Cifuentes and the professor, and monthly salaries for himself, the Chief Engineer of the *Juan Belmonte* and Teresa, the nude dancer. The drunken air-pilot was usually paid in whisky. The money Wormold accumulated he put into his deposit-account— one day it would make a dowry for Milly. Naturally to justify these payments he had to compose a regular supply of reports. With the help of a large map, the weekly number of *Time,* which gave generous space to Cuba in its section on the Western Hemisphere, various economic publications issued by the Government, above all with the help of his imagination, he had been able to arrange at least one report a week, and until the arrival of Beatrice he had kept his Saturday evenings free for homework. The professor was the economic authority, and Engineer Cifuentes dealt with the mysterious constructions in the mountains of Oriente (his reports were sometimes confirmed and sometimes contradicted by the Cubana pilot—a contradiction had a flavour of authenticity). The chief engineer supplied descriptions of labour conditions in Santiago, Matanzas and Cienfuegos and reported on the growth of unrest in the navy. As for the nude dancer, she supplied spicy details of the private lives and sexual eccentricities of the Defence Minister and the Director of Posts and Telegraphs. Her reports closely resembled articles about film stars in *Confidential,* for Wormold's imagination in this direction was not very strong.

Now that Beatrice was here, Wormold had a great deal more to worry about than his Saturday evening exercises. There was not only the basic training which Beatrice insisted on giving him in microphotography, there were also the cables he had to think up in order to keep Rudy happy, and the more cables Wormold sent the more he received. Every week now London bothered him for photographs of the installations in Oriente, and every week Beatrice became more impatient to take over the contact with his agents. It was against all the rules, she told him, for the head of a station to meet his own sources. Once he took her to dinner at the Country Club and, as bad luck would have it, Engineer Cifuentes was paged. A very tall lean man with a squint rose from a table near-by.

"Is that Cifuentes?" Beatrice asked sharply.

"Yes."

"But you told me he was sixty-five."

"He looks young for his age."

"And you said he had a paunch."

"Not paunch—ponch. It's the local dialect for squint."
It was a very narrow squeak.

After that she began to interest herself in a more
romantic figure of Wormold's imagination—the pilot of
Cubana. She worked enthusiastically to make his entry in
the index complete and wanted the most personal details.
Raul Dominguez certainly had pathos. He had lost his
wife in a massacre during the Spanish civil war and had
become disillusioned with both sides, with his Communist
friends in particular. The more Beatrice asked Wormold
about him, the more his character developed, and the
more anxious she became to contact him. Sometimes Wormold felt a twinge of jealousy towards Raul and he tried
to blacken the picture. "He gets through a bottle of
whisky a day," he said.

"It's his escape from loneliness and memory," Beatrice
said. "Don't *you* ever want to escape?"

"I suppose we all do sometimes."

"I know what that kind of loneliness is like," she said
with sympathy. "Does he drink all day?"

"No. The worst hour is two in the morning. When he
wakes then, he can't sleep for thinking, so he drinks
instead." It astonished Wormold how quickly he could
reply to any questions about his characters; they seemed
to live on the threshold of consciousness—he had only to
turn a light on and there they were, frozen in some
characteristic action. Soon after Beatrice arrived Raul had
a birthday and she suggested they should give him a case
of champagne.

"He won't touch it," Wormold said, he didn't know
why. "He suffers from acidity. If he drinks champagne he
comes out in spots. Now the professor on the other hand
won't drink anything else."

"An expensive taste."

"A depraved taste," Wormold said without taking any
thought. "He prefers Spanish champagne." Sometimes he
was scared at the way these people grew in the dark

without his knowledge. What was Teresa doing down there, out of sight? He didn't care to think. Her unabashed description of what life was like with her two lovers sometimes shocked him. But the immediate problem was Raul. There were moments when Wormold thought that it might have been easier if he had recruited real agents.

Wormold always thought best in his bath. He was aware one morning, when he was concentrating hard, of indignant noises, a fist beat on the door a number of times, somebody stamped on the stairs, but a creative moment had arrived and he paid no attention to the world beyond the steam. Raul had been dismissed by the Cubana air line for drunkenness. He was desperate; he was without a job; there had been an unpleasant interview between him and Captain Segura, who threatened . . .

"Are you all right?" Beatrice called from outside. "Are you dying? Shall I break down the door?"

He wrapped a towel round his middle and emerged into his bedroom, which was now his office.

"Milly went off in a rage," Beatrice said. "She missed her bath."

"This is one of those moments," Wormold said, "which might change the course of history. Where is Rudy?"

"You know you gave him week-end leave."

"Never mind. We'll have to send the cable through the Consulate. Get out the code-book."

"It's in the safe. What's the combination? Your birthday—that was it, wasn't it? December 6?"

"I changed it."

"Your birthday?"

"No, no. The combination, of course." He added sententiously, "'The fewer who know the combination the better for all of us. Rudy and I are quite sufficient. It's the drill, you know, that counts." He went into Rudy's room and began to twist the knob—four times to the left, three times thoughtfully to the right. His towel kept on slipping. "Besides, anyone can find out the date of my birth from my registration-card. Most unsafe. The sort of number they'd try at once."

"Go on," Beatrice said, "one more turn."

"This is one nobody could find out. Absolutely secure."

"What are you waiting for?"

"I must have made a mistake. I shall have to start again."

"This combination certainly seems secure."

"Please don't watch. You're fussing me." Beatrice went and stood with her face to the wall. She said, "Tell me when I can turn round again."

"It's very odd. The damn thing must have broken. Get Rudy on the phone."

"I can't. I don't know where he's staying. He's gone to Varadero beach."

"Damn!"

"Perhaps if you told me how you remembered the number, if you can call it remembering . . ."

"It was my great-aunt's telephone number."

"Where does she live?"

"95 Woodstock Road, Oxford."

"Why your great-aunt?"

"Why not my great-aunt?"

"I suppose we could put through a directory-enquiry to Oxford."

"'I doubt whether they could help."

"What's her name?"

"I've forgotten that too."

"The combination really is secure, isn't it?"

"We always just knew her as great-aunt Kate. Anyway she's been dead for fifteen years and the number may have been changed."

"I don't see why you chose her number."

"Don't you have a few numbers that stick in your head all your life for no reason at all?"

"This doesn't seem to have stuck very well."

"I'll remember it in a moment. It's something like 7, 7, 5, 3, 9."

"Oh dear, they would have five numbers in Oxford."

"We could try all the combinations of 77539."

"Do you know how many there are? Somewhere around six hundred I'd guess. I hope your cable's not urgent."

"I'm certain of everything except the 7."

"That's fine. Which seven? I suppose now we might have to work through about six thousand arrangements. I'm no mathematician."

"Rudy must have it written down somewhere."

"Probably on waterproof paper so that he can take it in with him bathing. We're an efficient office."

"Perhaps," Wormold said, "we had better use the old code."

"It's not very secure. However . . ." They found Charles Lamb at last by Milly's bed; a leaf turned down showed that she was in the middle of *Two Gentlemen of Verona*.

Wormold said, "Take down this cable. Blank of March blank."

"Don't you even know the day of the month?"

"Following from 59200 stroke 5 paragraph A begins 59200 stroke 5 stroke 4 sacked for drunkenness on duty stop fears deportation to Spain where his life is in danger stop."

"Poor old Raul."

"Paragraph B begins 59200 stroke 5 stroke 4 . . ."

"Couldn't I just say 'he'?"

"All right. He. He might be prepared under these circumstances and for reasonable bonus with assured refuge in Jamaica to pilot private plane over secret constructions to obtain photographs stop paragraph C begins he would have to fly on from Santiago and land at Kingston if 59200 can make arrangements for reception stop."

"We really are doing something at last, aren't we?" Beatrice said.

"Paragraph D begins stop will you authorise five hundred dollars for hire of plane for 59200 stroke 5 stroke 4 stop further two hundred dollars may be required to bribe airport staff Havana stop paragraph E begins bonus to 59200 stroke 5 stroke 4 should be generous as considerable risk of interception by patrolling planes over Oriente mountains stop I suggest one thousand dollars stop."

"What a lot of lovely money," Beatrice said.

"Message ends. Go on. What are you waiting for?"

"I'm just trying to find a suitable phrase. I don't much care for Lamb's *Tales*, do you?"

"Seventeen hundred dollars," Wormold said thoughtfully.

"You should have made it two thousand. The A.O. likes round figures."

"I don't want to seem extravagant," Wormold said. Seventeen hundred dollars would surely cover one year at a finishing school in Switzerland.

"You're looking pleased with yourself," Beatrice said. "Doesn't it occur to you that you may be sending a man to his death?" He thought, That is exactly what I plan to do.

He said, "Tell them at the Consulate that the cable has to have top priority."

"It's a long cable," Beatrice said. "Do you think this sentence will do? 'He presented Polydore and Cadwal to the king, telling him they were his two lost sons, Guiderius and Arviragus.' There are times, aren't there, when Shakespeare is a little dull."

ii

A week later he took Beatrice out to supper at a fish-restaurant near the harbour. The authorisation had come, though they had cut him down by two hundred dollars so that the A.O. got his round figure after all. Wormold thought of Raul driving out to the airport to embark on his dangerous flight. The story was not yet complete. Just as in real life, accidents could happen; a character might take control. Perhaps Raul would be intercepted before embarking, perhaps he would be stopped by a police-car on his way. He might disappear into the torture-chambers of Captain Segura. No reference would appear in the press. Wormold would warn London that he was going off the air in case Raul was forced to talk. The radio-set would be dismantled and hidden after the last message had been sent, the celluloid sheets would be kept ready for a final conflagration . . . Or perhaps Raul would take off in safety and they would never know what exactly happened to him over the Oriente mountains. Only one thing in the story was certain: he would not arrive in Jamaica and there would be no photographs.

"What are you thinking?" Beatrice asked. He hadn't touched his stuffed langouste.

"I was thinking of Raul." The wind blew up from the Atlantic. Moro Castle lay like a liner gale-bound across the harbour.

"Anxious?"

"Of course I'm anxious." If Raul had taken off at midnight, he would refuel just before dawn in Santiago, where the ground-staff were friendly, everyone within the Oriente province being rebels at heart. Then when it was just light enough for photography and too early for the patrol planes to be up, he would begin his reconaissance over the mountains and the forest.

"He hasn't been drinking?"

"He promised me he wouldn't. One can't tell."

"Poor Raul."

"Poor Raul."

"He's never had much fun, has he? You should have introduced him to Teresa."

He looked sharply up at her, but she seemed deeply engaged over her langouste.

"That wouldn't have been very secure, would it?"

"Oh, damn security," she said.

After supper they walked back along the landward side of the Avenida de Maceo. There were few people about in the wet windy night and little traffic. The rollers came in from the Atlantic and smashed over the sea-wall. The spray drove across the road, over the four traffic-lanes, and beat like rain under the pock-marked pillars where they walked. The clouds came racing from the east, and he felt himself to be part of the slow erosion of Havana. Fifteen years was a long time. He said, "One of those lights up there may be him. How solitary he must feel."

"You talk like a novelist," she said.

He stopped under a pillar and watched her with anxiety and suspicion.

"What do you mean?"

"Oh, nothing in particular. Sometimes I think you treat your agents like lay figures, people in a book. It's a real man up there—isn't it?"

"That's not a very nice thing to say about me."

"Oh, forget it. Tell me about someone you really care about. Your wife. Tell me about her."

"She was pretty."

"Do you miss her?"

"Of course. When I think of her."

"I don't miss Peter."

"Peter?"

"My husband. The UNESCO man."

"You're lucky then. You're free." He looked at his watch and the sky. "He should be over Matanzas by now. Unless he's been delayed."

"Have you sent him that way?"

"Oh, of course he decides his own route."

"And his own end?"

Something in her voice—a kind of enmity—startled him again. Was it possible she had begun to suspect him already? He walked quickly on. They passed the Carmen Bar and the Cha Cha Club—bright signs painted on the old shutters of the eighteenth-century façade. Lovely faces looked out of dim interiors, brown eyes, dark hair, Spanish and high yellow: beautiful buttocks leant against the bars, waiting for any life to come along the sea-wet street. To live in Havana was to live in a factory that turned out human beauty on a conveyor-belt. He didn't want beauty. He stopped under a lamp and looked directly back at the direct eyes. He wanted honesty. "Where are we going?"

"Don't you know? Isn't it all planned like Raul's flight?"

"I was just walking."

"Don't you want to sit beside the radio? Rudy's on duty."

"We won't have any news before the early morning."

"You haven't planned a late message then—the crash at Santiago?"

His lips were dry with salt and apprehension. It seemed to him that she must have guessed everything. Would she report him to Hawthorne? What would be "their" next move? They had no legal remedy, but he supposed they could stop him ever returning to England. He thought: She will go back by the next plane, life will be the same as before, and, of course, it was better that way; his life belonged to Milly. He said, "I don't understand what you mean." A great wave had broken against the sea-wall of the Avenida, and now it rose like a Christmas-tree covered with plastic frost. Then it sank out of sight, and another tree rose further down the driveway towards the Nacional. He said, "You've been strange all the evening." There was no point in delay; if the game were coming to an end, it was better to close it quickly. He said, "What are you hinting at?"

"You mean there isn't to be a crash at the airport—or on the way?"

"How do you expect me to know?"

"You've been behaving all the evening as if you did. You haven't spoken about him as though he were a living man. You've been writing his elegy like a bad novelist preparing an effect."

The wind knocked them together. She said, "Aren't you ever tired of other people taking risks? For what? For a *Boys' Own Paper* game?"

"You play the game."

"I don't believe in it like Hawthorne does." She said furiously, "I'd rather be a crook than a simpleton or an adolescent. Don't you earn enough with your vacuum cleaners to keep out of all this?"

"No. There's Milly."

"Suppose Hawthorne hadn't walked in on you?"

He joked miserably, "Perhaps I'd have married again for money."

"Would you ever marry again?" She seemed determined to be serious.

"Well," he said, "I don't know that I would. Milly

wouldn't consider it a marriage, and one can't shock one's own child. Shall we go home and listen to the radio?"

"But you don't expect a message, do you? You said so."

He said evasively, "Not for another three hours. But I expect he'll radio before he lands." The odd thing was he began to feel the tension. He almost hoped for some message to reach him out of the windy sky.

She said, "Will you promise me that you haven't ar- ranged—anything?"

He avoided answering, turning back towards the Pres- ident's palace with the dark windows where the President had never slept since the last attempt on his life, and there, coming down the pavement with head bent to avoid the spray, was Dr. Hasselbacher. He was probably on his way home from the Wonder Bar.

"Dr. Hasselbacher," Wormold called to him.

The old man looked up. For a moment Wormold thought he was going to turn tail without a word. "What's the matter, Hasselbacher?"

"Oh, it's you, Mr. Wormold. I was just thinking of you. Talk of the devil," he said, making a joke of it, but Wormold could have sworn that the devil had scared him.

"You remember Mrs. Severn, my secretary?"

"The birthday party, yes, and the siphon. What are you doing up so late, Mr. Wormold?"

"We've been out to supper . . . a walk . . . and you?"

"The same thing."

Out of the vast tossing sky the sound of an engine came spasmodically down, increased, faded again, died out into the noise of wind and sea. Dr. Hasselbacher said, "The plane from Santiago, but it's very late. The weather must be bad in Oriente."

"Are you expecting anyone?" Wormold asked.

"No. No. Not expecting. Would you and Mrs. Severn care to have a drink at my apartment?"

Violence had come and gone. The pictures were back in place, the tubular chairs stood around like awkward guests. The apartment had been reconstructed like a man for burial. Dr. Hasselbacher poured out the whisky.

"It is nice for Mr. Wormold to have a secretary," he said. "Such a short time ago you were worried, I remember. Business was not so good. That new cleaner . . ."

"Things change for no reason."

He noticed for the first time the photograph of a young Dr. Hasselbacher in the dated uniform of an officer in the First World War; perhaps it had been one of the pictures the intruders had taken off the wall. "I never knew you had been in the army, Hasselbacher."

"I had not finished my medical training, Mr. Wormold, when the war came. It struck me as a very silly business—curing men so that they could be killed sooner. One wanted to cure people so that they could live longer."

"When did you leave Germany, Dr. Hasselbacher?" Beatrice asked.

"In 1934. So I can plead not guilty, young lady, to what you are wondering."

"That was not what I meant."

"You must forgive me then. Ask Mr. Wormold—there was a time when I was not so suspicious. Shall we have some music?"

He put on a record of *Tristan*. Wormold thought of his wife; she was even less real than Raul. She had nothing to do with love and death, only with the *Woman's Home Journal*, a diamond engagement ring, twilight-sleep. He looked across the room at Beatrice Severn, and she seemed to him to belong to the same world as the fatal drink, the hopeless journey from Ireland, the surrender in the forest. Abruptly Dr. Hasselbacher stood up and pulled the plug from the wall. He said, "Forgive me. I am expecting a call. The music is too loud."

"A sick call?"

"Not exactly." He poured out more whiskey.

"Have you started your experiments again, Hasselbacher?"

"No." He looked despairingly around. "I am sorry. There is no more soda water."

"I like it straight," Beatrice said. She went to the bookshelf. "Do you read anything but medical books, Dr. Hasselbacher?"

"Very little. Heine, Goethe. All German. Do you read German, Mrs. Severn?"

"No. But you have a few English books."

"They were given me by a patient instead of a fee. I'm afraid I haven't read them. Here is your whisky, Mrs. Severn."

She came away from the bookcase and took the whisky. "Is that your home, Dr. Hasselbacher?" She was looking at a Victorian coloured lithograph hanging beside young Captain Hasselbacher's portrait.

"I was born there. Yes. It is a very small town, some old walls, a castle in ruins . . ."

"I've been there," Beatrice said, "before the war. My father took us. It's near Leipzig, isn't it?"

"Yes, Mrs. Severn," Dr. Hasselbacher said, watching her bleakly, "it is near Leipzig."

"I hope the Russians left it undisturbed."

The telephone in Dr. Hasselbacher's hall began to ring. He hesitated a moment. "Excuse me, Mrs. Severn," he said. When he went into the hall he shut the door behind him. "East or west," Beatrice said, "home's best."

"I suppose you want to report that to London? But I've known him for fifteen years, he's lived here for more than twenty. He's a good old man, the best friend . . ." The door opened and Dr. Hasselbacher returned. He said, "I'm sorry. I don't feel very well. Perhaps you will come and hear music some other evening." He sat heavily down, picked up his whisky, put it back again. There was sweat on his forehead, but after all it was a humid night.

"Bad news?" Wormold asked.

"Yes."

"Can I help?"

"You!" Dr. Hasselbacher said. "No. *You* can't help. Or Mrs. Severn."

"A patient?" Dr. Hasselbacher shook his head. He took out his handkerchief and dried his forehead. He said, "Who is not a patient?"

"We'd better go."

"Yes, go. It is like I said. One ought to be able to cure people so that they can live longer."

"I don't understand."

"Was there never such a thing as peace?" Dr. Hasselbacher asked. "I am sorry. A doctor is always supposed to get used to death. But I am not a good doctor."

"Who has died?"

"There has been an accident," Dr. Hasselbacher said. "Just an accident. Of course an accident. A car has crashed on the road near the airport. A young man . . ." He said furiously, "There are always accidents, aren't there, everywhere. And this must surely have been an accident. He was too fond of the glass."

Beatrice said, "Was his name by any chance Raul?"

"Yes," Dr. Hasselbacher said. "That was his name."

PART IV

[1]

i

Wormold unlocked the door. The street-lamp over the way vaguely disclosed the vacuum cleaners standing around like tombs. He started for the stairs. Beatrice whispered, "Stop, stop. I thought I heard . . ." They were the first words either of them had spoken since he had shut the door of Dr. Hasselbacher's apartment.

"What's the matter?"

She put out a hand and clutched some metallic part from the counter; she held it like a club and said, "I'm frightened."

Not half as much as I am, he thought. Can we write human beings into existence? And what sort of existence? Had Shakespeare listened to the news of Duncan's death in a tavern or heard the knocking on his own bedroom door after he had finished the writing of *Macbeth?* He stood in the shop and hummed a tune to keep his courage up.

> They say the earth is round—
> My madness offends.

"Quiet," Beatrice said. "Somebody's moving upstairs."

He thought he was afraid only of his own imaginary characters, not of a living person who could creak a board. He ran up and was stopped abruptly by a shadow. He was tempted to call out to all his creations at once and have done with the lot of them—Teresa, the chief, the professor, the engineer.

"How late you are," Milly's voice said. It was only Milly standing there in the passage between the lavatory and her room.

"We went for a walk."

"You brought her back?" Milly asked. "Why?"

Beatrice cautiously climbed the stairs, holding her improvised club on guard.

"Is Rudy awake?"

"I don't think so."

Beatrice said, "If there'd been a message, he would have sat up for you."

If one's characters were alive enough to die, they were surely real enough to send messages. He opened the door of the office. Rudy stirred.

"Any message, Rudy?"

"No."

Milly said, "You've missed all the excitement."

"What excitement?"

"The police were dashing everywhere. You should have heard the sirens. I though it was a revolution, so I rang up Captain Segura."

"Yes?"

"Someone tried to assassinate someone as he came out of the Ministry of the Interior. He must have thought it was the Minister, only it wasn't. He shot out of a car-window and got clean away."

"Who was it?"

"They haven't caught him yet."

"I mean the—the assassinee."

"Nobody important. But he looked like the Minister. Where did you have supper?"

"The Victoria."

"Did you have stuffed langouste?"

"Yes."

"I'm so glad you don't look like the President. Captain Segura said poor Dr. Cifuentes was so scared he went and wet his trousers and then got drunk at the Country Club."

"Dr. Cifuentes?"

"You know—the engineer."

"They shot at him?"

"I told you it was a mistake."

"Let's sit down," Beatrice said. She spoke for both of them.

He said, "The dining-room . . ."

"I don't want a hard chair. I want something soft. I may want to cry."

"Well, if you don't mind the bedroom," he said doubtfully, looking at Milly.

"Did you know Dr. Cifuentes?" Milly asked Beatrice sympathetically.

"No. I only know he has a ponch."

"What's a ponch?"

"Your father said it was a dialect word for a squint."

"He told you that? Poor Father," Milly said. "You *are* in deep waters."

"Look, Milly, will you please go to bed? Beatrice and I have work to do."

"Work?"

"Yes, work."

"It's awfully late for work."

"He's paying me overtime," Beatrice said.

"Are you learning all about vacuum cleaners?" Milly asked. "That thing you are holding is a sprayer."

"Is it? I just picked it up in case I had to hit someone."

"It's not well suited for that," Milly said. "It has a telescopic tube."

"What if it has?"

"It might telescope at the wrong moment."

"Milly, please . . ." Wormold said. "It's nearly two."

"Don't worry. I'm off. And I shall pray for Dr. Cifuentes. It's no joke to be shot at. The bullet went right through a brick wall. Think of what it could have done to Dr. Cifuentes."

"Pray for someone called Raul too," Beatrice said. "They got *him*."

Wormold lay down flat on the bed and shut his eyes. "I don't understand a thing," he said. "Not a thing. It's a coincidence. It must be."

"They're getting rough—whoever they are."

"But why?"

"Spying is a dangerous profession."

"But Cifuentes hadn't really . . . I mean he wasn't important."

"Those constructions in Oriente are important. Your agents seem to have a habit of getting blown. I wonder how. I think you'll have to warn Professor Sanchez and the girl."

"The girl?"

"The nude dancer."

"But how?" He couldn't explain to her he had no agents, that he had never met Cifuentes or Dr. Sanchez, that neither Teresa nor Raul even existed: Raul had come alive only in order to be killed.

"What did Milly call this?"

"A sprayer."

"I've seen something like it before somewhere."

"I expect you have. Most vacuum cleaners have them." He took it away from her. He couldn't remember whether he had included it in the drawings he had sent to Hawthorne.

"What do I do now, Beatrice?"

"I think your people should go into hiding for a while. Not here, of course. It would be too crowded and anyway not safe. What about that Chief Engineer of yours—could he smuggle them on board?"

"He's away at sea on the way to Cienfuegos."

"Anyway he's probably blown too," she said thoughtfully. "I wonder why they've let you and me get back here."

"What do you mean?"

"They could easily have shot us down on the front. Or perhaps they're using us for bait. Of course you throw away the bait if it's no good."

"What a macabre woman you are."

"Oh no. We're back into the *Boy's Own Paper* world, that's all. You can count yourself lucky."

"Why?"

"It might have been the *Sunday Mirror*. The world is modelled after the popular magazines nowadays. My husband came out of *Encounter*. The question we have to consider is to which paper *they* belong."

"They?"

"Let's assume they belong to the *Boy's Own Paper* too. Are they Russian agents, German agents, American, what? Cuban very likely. Those concrete platforms must be official, mustn't they? Poor Raul. I hope he died quickly."

He was tempted to tell her everything, but what was "everything"? He no longer knew. Raul had been killed. Hasselbacher said so.

"First the Shanghai Theatre," she said. "Will it be open?"

"The second performance won't be over."

"If the police are not there before us. Of course they didn't use the police against Cifuentes. He was probably too important. In murdering anyone you have to avoid scandal."

"I hadn't thought of it in that light before."

Beatrice turned out the bedside light and went to the window. She said, "Don't you have a back door?"

"No."

"We'll have to change all that," she said airily, as though she were an architect too. "Do you know a nigger with a limp?"

"That will be Joe."

"He's going slowly by."

"He sells dirty postcards. He's going home, that's all."

"He couldn't be expected to follow you with that limp, of course. He may be their tictac man. Anyway we'll have to risk it. They are obviously making a sweep tonight. Women and children first. The professor can wait."

"But I've never seen Teresa at the theatre. She probably has a different name there."

"You can pick her out, can't you, even without her clothes? Though I suppose we do look a bit the same naked, like the Japanese."

"I don't think you ought to come."

"I must. If one is stopped the other can make a dash for it."

"I meant to the Shanghai. It's not exactly *Boy's Own Paper*."

"Nor is marriage," she said, "even in UNESCO."

ii

The Shanghai was in a narrow street off Zanja surrounded by deep bars. A board advertised *Posiciones,* and the tickets for some reason were sold on the pavement outside, perhaps because there was no room for a box-office, as the foyer was occupied by a pornographic bookshop for the benefit of those who wanted entertainment during the *entr'acte*. The black pimps in the street watched them with curiosity. They were not used to European women here.

"It feels far from home," Beatrice said.

The seats all cost one peso twenty-five and there were very few empty ones left in the large hall. The man who showed them the way offered Wormold a packet of pornographic postcards for a peso. When Wormold refused them, he drew a second selection from his pocket.

"Buy them if you want to," Beatrice said. "If it embarrasses you I'll keep my eye on the show."

"There's not much difference," Wormold said, "between the show and the postcards."

The attendant asked if the lady would like a marijuana cigarette.

"Nein, danke," Beatrice said, getting her languages confused.

On either side of the stage, posters advertised clubs in the neighbourhood where the girls were said to be beautiful. A notice in Spanish and bad English forbade the audience to molest the dancers.

"Which is Teresa?" Beatrice asked.

"I think it must be the fat one in the mask," Wormold said at random.

She was just leaving the stage with a heave of her great naked buttocks, and the audience clapped and whistled. Then the lights went down and a screen was lowered. A film began, quite mildly at first. It showed a bicyclist,

some woodland scenery, a punctured tyre, a chance encounter, a gentleman raising a straw hat; there was a
great deal of flicker and fog.

Beatrice sat silent. There was an odd intimacy between
them as they watched together this blueprint of love.
Similar movements of the body had once meant more to
them than anything else the world had to offer. The act of
lust and the act of love are the same; it cannot be falsified
like a sentiment.

The lights went on. They sat in silence. "My lips are
dry," Wormold said.

"I haven't any spit left. Can't we go behind and see
Teresa now?"

"There's another film after this and then the dancers
come on again."

"I'm not tough enough for another film," Beatrice
said.

"They won't let us go behind until the show's over."

"We can wait in the street, can't we? At least we'll know
then if we've been followed."

They left as the second film started. They were the only
ones to rise, so if somebody had tailed them he must be
waiting for them in the street, but there was no obvious
candidate among the taxi-drivers and the pimps. One man
slept against the lamp-post with a lottery-number slung
askew round his neck. Wormold remembered the night
with Dr. Hasselbacher. That was when he had learnt the
new use for Lamb's *Tales from Shakespeare*. Poor Hasselbacher had been very drunk. Wormold remembered
how he had sat slumped in the lounge when he came
down from Hawthorne's room. He said to Beatrice, "How
easy is it to break a book-code if once you've got the right
book?"

"Not hard for an expert," she said, "only a question of
patience." She went across to the lottery-seller and
straightened the number. The man didn't wake. She said,
"It was difficult to read it sideways."

Had he carried Lamb under his arm, in his pocket, or
in his brief-case? Had he laid the book down when he

helped Dr. Hasselbacher to rise? He could remember nothing, and such suspicions were ungenerous.

"I thought of a funny coincidence," Beatrice said. "Dr. Hasselbacher reads Lamb's *Tales* in the right edition." It was as though her basic training had included telepathy.

"You saw it in his flat?"

"Yes."

"But he would have hidden it," he protested, "if it meant anything at all."

"Or he wanted to warn you. Remember, he brought us back there. He told us about Raul."

"He couldn't have known that he would meet us."

"How do you know?"

He wanted to protest that nothing made sense, that Raul didn't exist, and that Teresa didn't exist, and then he thought of how she would pack up and go away and it would all be like a story without a purpose.

"People are coming out," Beatrice said.

They found a side-door that led to the one big dressing-room. The passage was lit by a bare globe that had burned far too many days and nights. The passage was nearly blocked by dustbins and a negro with a broom was sweeping up scraps of cotton-wool stained with face powder, lipstick and ambiguous things; the place smelled of pear-drops. Perhaps after all there would be no one here called Teresa, but he wished that he had not chosen so popular a saint. He pushed a door open and it was like a medieval inferno full of smoke and naked women.

He said to Beatrice, "Don't you think you'd better go home?"

"It's you who need protection here," she said.

Nobody even noticed them. The mask of the fat woman dangled from one ear and she was drinking a glass of wine with one leg up on a chair. A very thin girl with ribs like piano-keys was pulling on her stockings. Breasts swayed, buttocks bent, cigarettes half finished fumed in saucers; the air was thick with burning paper. A man stood on a stepladder with a screwdriver fixing something.

"Where is she?" Beatrice asked.

"I don't think she's here. Perhaps she's sick, or with her lover."

The air flapped warmly round them as someone put on a dress. Little grains of powder settled like ash.

"Try calling her name."

He shouted "Teresa" half-heartedly. Nobody paid any attention. He tried again and the man with the screwdriver looked down at him.

"Paso algo?" he asked.

Wormold said in Spanish that he was looking for a girl called Teresa. The man suggested that Maria would do just as well. He pointed his screwdriver at the fat woman.

"What's he saying?"

"He doesn't seem to know Teresa."

The man with the screwdriver sat down on top of the ladder and began to make a speech. He said that Maria was the best woman you could find in Havana. She weighed one hundred kilos with nothing on.

"Obviously Teresa is not here," Wormold explained with relief.

"Teresa. Teresa. What do you want with Teresa?"

"Yes. What do you want with me?" the thin girl demanded, coming forward holding out one stocking. Her little breasts were the size of pears.

"Who are you?"

"Soy Teresa."

Beatrice said, "Is that Teresa? You said she was fat—like that one with the mask."

"No, no," Wormold said. "That's not Teresa. She's Teresa's sister. *Soy* means sister." He said, "I'll send a message by her." He took the thin girl's arm and moved her a little away. He tried to explain to her in Spanish that she had to be careful.

"Who are you? I don't understand."

"There has been a mistake. It is too long a story. There are people who may try to do you an injury. Please stay at home for a few days. Don't come to the theatre."

"I have to. I meet my clients here."

Wormold took out a wad of money. He said, "Have you relations?"

"I have my mother."

"Go to her."

"But she is in Cienfuegos."

"There is plenty of money there to take you to Cienfuegos." Everybody was listening now. They pressed close around. The man with the screwdriver had come down from the ladder. Wormold saw Beatrice outside the circle; she was pushing closer, trying to make out what he was saying.

The man with the screwdriver said, "That girl belongs to Pedro. You can't take her away like that. You must talk to Pedro first."

"I do not want to go to Cienfuegos," the girl said.

"You will be safe there."

She appealed to the man. "He frightens me. I cannot understand what he wants." She exhibited the pesos. "This is too much money." She appealed to them. "I am a good girl."

"A lot of wheat does not make a bad year," the fat woman said with solemnity.

"Where is your Pedro?" the man asked.

"He is ill. Why does the man give me all this money? I am a good girl. You know that my price is fifteen pesos. I am not a hustler."

"A lean dog is full of fleas," said the fat woman. She seemed to have a proverb for every occasion.

"What's happening?" Beatrice asked.

A voice hissed, "Psst, psst!" It was the negro who had been sweeping the passage. He said, *"Policia!"*

"Oh hell," Wormold said, "that tears it. I've got to get you out of here." No one seemed unduly disturbed. The fat woman drained her wine and put on a pair of knickers; the girl who was called Teresa pulled on her second stocking.

"It doesn't matter about me," Beatrice said. "You've got to get *her* away."

"What do the police want?" Wormold asked the man on the ladder.

"A girl," he said cynically.

"I want to get this girl out," Wormold said. "Isn't there some back way?"

"With the police there's always a back way."

"Where?"

"Got fifty pesos to spare?"

"Yes."

"Give them to him. Hi, Miguel," he called to the negro. "Tell them to stay asleep for three minutes. Now who wants to be treated to freedom?"

"I prefer the police-station," the fat woman said. "But one has to be properly clothed." She adjusted her bra.

"Come with me," Wormold said to Teresa.

"Why should I?"

"You don't realise—they want you."

"I doubt it," said the man with the screwdriver. "She's too thin. You had better hurry. Fifty pesos do not last for ever."

"Here, take my coat," Beatrice said. She wrapped it round the shoulders of the girl, who had now two stockings on but nothing else. The girl said, "But I want to stay."

The man slapped her bottom and gave her a push. "You have his money," he said. "Go with him." He herded them into a small and evil toilet and then through a window. They found themselves in the street. A policeman on guard outside the theatre ostentatiously looked elsewhere. A pimp whistled and pointed to Wormold's car. The girl said again, "I want to stay," but Beatrice pushed her into the rear seat and followed her in. "I shall scream," the girl told them and leant out of the window.

"Don't be a fool," Beatrice said, pulling her inside. Wormold got the car started.

The girl screamed but only in a tentative way. The policeman turned and looked in the opposite direction. The fifty pesos seemed to be still effective. They turned right and drove towards the sea-front. No car followed them. It was as easy as all that. The girl, now that she had no choice, adjusted the coat for modesty and leant comfortably back. She said, *"Hay mucha corriente."*

"What's she saying?"

"She's complaining of the draught," Wormold said.

"She doesn't seem a very grateful girl. Where's her sister?"

"With the Director of Posts and Telegraphs, at Cienfuegos. Of course I could drive her there. We'd arrive by breakfast time. But there's Milly."

"There's more than Milly. You've forgotten Professor Sanchez."

"Surely Professor Sanchez can wait."

"They seem to be acting fast, whoever they are."

"I don't know where he lives."

"I do. I looked him up in the Country Club list before we came."

"You take this girl home and wait there."

They came out on to the front. "You turn left here," Beatrice said.

"I'm taking you home."

"It's better to stay together."

"Milly . . ."

"You don't want to compromise *her,* do you?"

Reluctantly Wormold turned left. "Where to?"

"Vedado," Beatrice said.

iii

The skyscrapers of the new town stood up ahead of them like icicles in the moonlight. A great H.H. was stamped on the sky, like the monogram on Hawthorne's pocket, but it wasn't royal either—it only advertised Mr. Hilton. The wind rocked the car, and the spray broke across the traffic-lanes and misted the seaward window. The hot night tasted of salt. Wormold swung the car away from the sea. The girl said, *"Hace demasiado calor."*

"What's she saying now?"

"She says it's too hot."

"She's a difficult girl," Beatrice said. "Better turn down the window again."

"Suppose she screams?"

"I'll slap her."

They were in the new quarter of Vedado: little cream-and-white houses owned by rich men. You could tell how rich a man was by the fewness of the floors. Only a millionaire could afford a bungalow on a site that might have held a skyscraper. When he lowered the window they could smell the flowers. She stopped him by a gate in a high white wall. She said, "I can see lights in the patio. Everything seems all right. I'll guard your precious bit of flesh while you go in."

"He seems to be very wealthy for a professor."

"He's not too rich to charge expenses, according to your accounts."

Wormold said, "Give me a few minutes. Don't go away."

"Am I likely to? You'd better hurry. So far they've only scored one out of three, and a near miss, of course."

He tried the grilled gate. It was not locked. The position was absurd. How was he to explain his presence? "You are an agent of mine without knowing it. You are in danger. You must hide." He didn't even know of what subject Sanchez was a professor.

A short path between two palm-trees led to a second grilled gate, and beyond was the little patio where the lights were on. A gramophone was playing softly and two tall figures revolved in silence cheek to cheek. As he limped up the path a concealed alarm-bell rang. The dancers stopped and one of them came out on to the path to meet him.

"Who is that?"

"Professor Sanchez?"

"Yes."

They both converged into the area of light. The professor wore a white dinner-jacket, his hair was white, he had white morning stubble on his chin, and he carried a revolver in his hand which he pointed at Wormold. Wormold saw that the woman behind him was very young and very pretty. She stooped and turned off the gramophone.

"Forgive me for calling on you at this hour," Wormold said. He had no idea how he should begin, and he was disquieted by the revolver. Professors ought not to carry revolvers.

"I am afraid I don't remember your face." The professor spoke politely and kept the revolver pointed at Wormold's stomach.

"There's no reason why you should. Unless you have a vacuum cleaner."

"Vacuum cleaner? I suppose I have. Why? My wife would know." The young woman came through from the patio and joined them. She had no shoes on. The discarded shoes stood beside the gramophone like mouse-traps. "What does he want?" she asked disagreeably.

"I'm sorry to disturb you, Señora Sanchez."

"Tell him I'm not Señora Sanchez," the young woman said.

"He says he has something to do with vacuum cleaners," the professor said. "Do you think Maria, before she went away . . . ?"

"Why does he come here at one in the morning?"

"You must forgive me," the professor said with an air of embarrassment, "but this *is* an unusual time." He allowed his revolver to move a little off target. "One doesn't as a rule expect visitors . . ."

"You seem to expect them."

"Oh, this—one has to take precautions. You see, I have some very fine Renoirs."

"He's not after the pictures. Maria sent him. You are a spy, aren't you?" the young woman asked fiercely.

"Well, in a way."

The young woman began to wail, beating at her own long slim flanks. Her bracelets jangled and glinted.

"Don't, dear, don't. I'm sure there's an explanation."

"She envies our happiness," the young woman said. "First she sent the cardinal, didn't she, and now this man . . . Are you a priest?" she asked.

"My dear, of course he's not a priest. Look at his clothes."

"You may be a professor of comparative education,"

the young woman said, "but you can be deceived by anyone. Are you a priest?" she repeated.

"No."

"What are you?"

"As a matter of fact I sell vacuum cleaners."

"You said you were a spy."

"Well, yes, I suppose in a sense . . ."

"What have you come here for?"

"To warn you."

The young woman gave an odd bitch-like howl. "You see," she said to the professor, "she's threatening us now. First the cardinal and then . . ."

"The cardinal was only doing his duty. After all he's Maria's cousin."

"You're afraid of him. You want to leave me."

"My dear, you know that isn't true." He said to Wormold, "Where is Maria now?"

"I don't know."

"When did you see her last?"

"But I've never seen her."

"You do rather contradict yourself, don't you?"

"He's a lying hound," the young woman said.

"Not necessarily, dear. he's probably employed by some agency. We had better sit down quietly and hear what he has to say. Anger is always a mistake. He's doing his duty—which is more than can be said of us." The professor led the way back to the patio. He had put his revolver back in his pocket. The young woman waited until Wormold began to follow and then brought up the rear like a watchdog. He half expected her to bite his ankle. He thought, Unless I speak soon, I shall never speak.

"Take a chair," the professor said. What *was* comparative education?

"May I give you a drink?"

"Please don't bother."

"You don't drink on duty?"

"Duty!" the young woman said. "You treat him like a human being. What duty has he got except to his despicable employers?"

"I came here to warn you that the police . . ."

"Oh come, come, adultery is not a crime," the professor said. "I think it has seldom been regarded as that except in the American colonies in the seventeenth century. And in the Mosaic Law, of course."

"Adultery has got nothing to do with it," the young woman said. "She didn't mind us sleeping together, she only minded our being together."

"You can hardly have one without the other, unless you are thinking of the New Testament," the professor said. "Adultery in the heart."

"You have no heart unless you turn this man out. We sit here talking as though we had been married for years. If all you want to do is to sit up all night and talk, why didn't you stick to Maria?"

"My dear, it was your idea to dance before bed."

"You call what you did dancing?"

"I told you that I would take lessons."

"Oh yes, so as to be with the girls at the school."

The conversation seemed to Wormold to be reeling out of sight. He said desperately, "They shot at Engineer Cifuentes. You are in the same danger."

"If I wanted girls, dear, there are plenty at the university. They come to my lectures. No doubt you are aware of that, since you came yourself."

"You taunt me with it?"

"We are straying from the subject, dear. The subject is what action Maria is likely to take next."

"She ought to have given up starchy foods two years ago," the young girl said rather cheaply, "knowing you. You only care for the body. You ought to be ashamed at your age."

"If you don't wish me to love you . . ."

"Love. Love." The young woman began to pace the patio. She made gestures in the air as though she were dismembering love. Wormold said, "It's not Maria you have to worry about."

"You lying hound," she screamed at him. "You said you'd never seen her."

"I haven't."

"Then why do you call her Maria?" she cried and began to do triumphant dance-steps with an imaginary partner.

"You said something about Cifuentes, young man?"

"He was shot at this evening."

"Who by?"

"I don't know exactly, but it's all part of the same round-up. It's a bit difficult to explain, but you really seem to be in great danger, Professor Sanchez. It's all a mistake, of course. The police have been to the Shanghai Theatre too."

"What have I to do with the Shanghai Theatre?"

"What indeed?" cried the young woman melodramatically. "Men," she said, "men! Poor Maria. She hasn't only one woman to deal with. She'll have to plan a massacre."

"I've never had anything to do with anybody at the Shanghai Theatre."

"Maria is better informed. I expect you walk in your sleep."

"You heard what he said, it's a mistake. After all, they shot at Cifuentes. You can't blame her for that."

"Cifuentes? Did he say Cifuentes? Oh, you Spanish oaf. Just because he talked to me one day at the Club while you were in the shower you go and hire desperadoes to kill him."

"Please, dear, be reasonable. I only heard of it just now when this gentleman . . ."

"He's not a gentleman. He's a lying hound." They had again come full circle in the conversation.

"If he's a liar we need pay no attention to what he says. He's probably slandering Maria too."

"Ah, you would stick up for her."

Wormold said with desperation—it was his last fling, "This has got nothing to do with Maria—with Señora Sanchez, I mean."

"What on earth has Señora Sanchez to do with it?" the professor asked.

"I thought you thought that Maria . . ."

"Young man, you aren't seriously telling me that Maria is planning to do something to my wife as well as to my . . . my friend here? It's too absurd."

Until now the mistake had seemed to Wormold fairly simple to deal with. But now it was as though he had tugged a stray piece of cotton and a whole suit had begun to unwind. Was this Comparative Education? He said, "I thought I was doing you a favour by coming to warn you, but it looks as if death for you might be the best solution."

"You are a very mystifying young man."

"Not young. It's you, Professor, who are young by the look of things." In his anxiety he spoke aloud, "If only Beatrice were here."

The professor said quickly, "I absolutely assure you, dear, that I know nobody called Beatrice. Nobody."

The young woman gave a tigerish laugh.

"You seem to have come here," the professor said, "with the sole purpose of making trouble." It was his first complaint and it seemed a very mild one under the circumstances. "I cannot think what you have to gain by it," he said and walked into the house and closed the door.

"He's a monster," the girl said. "A monster. A sexual monster. A satyr."

"You don't understand."

"I know that tag—to know all is to forgive all. Not in this case, it isn't." She seemed to have lost her hostility to Wormold. "Maria, me, Beatrice—I don't count his wife, poor woman. I've got nothing against his wife. Have you a gun?"

"Of course not. I only came to save him," Wormold said.

"Let them shoot," the young woman said, "in the belly —low down." And she too went into the house with an air of purpose.

There was nothing left for Wormold to do but go. The invisible alarm gave another warning as he walked towards the gate, but no one stirred in tthe little white house. I've done my best, Wormold thought. The professor seemed well prepared for any danger and perhaps the arrival of the police might be a relief to him. They would be easier to cope with than the young woman.

iv

Walking away through the smell of the night-flowering plants he had only one wish: to tell Beatrice everything. I am no secret agent, I'm a fraud, none of these people are my agents, and I don't know what's happening. I'm lost. I'm scared. Surely somehow she would take control of the situation; after all she was a professional. But he knew that he would not appeal to her. It meant giving up security for Milly. He would rather be eliminated like Raul. Did they, in his service, give pensions to offspring? But who was Raul?

Before he had reached the second gate Beatrice called to him, "Jim. Look out. Keep away." Even at that urgent moment the thought occurred to him, my name is Wormold, Mr. Wormold, Señor Vomel, nobody calls me Jim. Then he ran—hop and skip—towards the voice and came out to the street, to a radio-car, and to three police-officers, and another revolver pointing at his stomach. Beatrice stood on the sidewalk and the girl was beside her, trying to keep a coat closed which hadn't been designed that way.

"What's the matter?"

"I can't understand a word they say."

One of the officers told him to get into their car.

"What about my own?"

"It will be brought to the station." Before he obeyed they felt him down the breast and side for arms. He said to Beatrice, "I don't know what it's all about, but it looks like the end of a bright career." The officer spoke again. "He wants you to get in too."

"Tell him," Beatrice said, "I'm going to stay with Teresa's sister. I don't trust them."

The two cars drove softly away among the little houses of the millionaires, to avoid disturbing anyone, as though they were in a street of hospitals; the rich need sleep.

They had not far to go: a courtyard, a gate closing behind them, and then the odour of a police-station like the ammoniac smell of zoos all the world over. Along the whitewashed passage the portraits of wanted men hung, with the spurious look of bearded old masters. In the room at the end Captain Segura sat playing draughts. "Huff," he said, and took two pieces. Then he looked up at them. "Mr. Wormold," he said with surprise, and rose like a small tight green snake from his seat when he saw Beatrice. He looked beyond her at Teresa; the coat had fallen open again, perhaps with intention. He said, "Who in God's name . . . ?" and then to the policeman with whom he had been playing, *"Anda!"*

"What's the meaning of all this, Captain Segura?"

"You are asking me that, Mr. Wormold?"

"Yes."

"I wish you would tell me the meaning. I had no idea I should see you—Milly's father. Mr. Wormold, we had a call from a Professor Sanchez about a man who had broken into his house with vague threats. He thought it had something to do with his pictures; he has very valu- able pictures. I sent a radio-car at once and it is you they pick up, with the señorita here (we have met before) and a naked tart." Like the police-sergeant in Santiago he added, "That is not very nice, Mr. Wormold."

"We had been at the Shanghai."

"That is not very nice either."

"I'm tired of being told by the police that I am not nice."

"Why did you visit Professor Sanchez?"

"That was all a mistake."

"Why do you have a naked tart in your car?"

"We were giving her a lift."

"She has no right to be naked on the streets." The police-officer leant across the desk and whispered. "Ah," Captain Segura said. "I begin to understand. There was a police-inspection tonight at the Shanghai. I suppose the girl had forgotten her papers and wanted to avoid a night in the cells. She appealed to you . . ."

"It wasn't that way at all."

"It had better be that way, Mr. Wormold." He said to the girl in Spanish, "Your papers. You have no papers."

She said indignantly, *"Si, yo tengo."* She bent down and pulled pieces of crumpled paper from the top of her stockings. Captain Segura took them and examined them. He gave a deep sigh. "Mr. Wormold, Mr. Wormold, her papers are in order. Why do you drive about the streets with a naked girl? Why do you break into the house of Professor Sanchez and talk to him about his wife and threaten him? What is his wife to you?" He said "Go" sharply to the girl. She hesitated and began to take off the coat.

"Better let her keep it," Beatrice said.

Captain Segura sat wearily down in front of the draughts board. "Mr. Wormold, for your sake I tell you this: do not get mixed up with the wife of Professor Sanchez. She is not a woman you can treat lightly."

"I am not mixed up . . ."

"Do you play checkers, Mr. Wormold?"

"Yes. Not very well, I'm afraid."

"Better than these pigs in the station, I expect. We must play together sometimes, you and I. But in checkers you must move very carefully, just as with the wife of Professor Sanchez." He moved a piece at random on the board and said, "Tonight you were with Dr. Hasselbacher."

"Yes."

"Was that wise, Mr. Wormold?" He didn't look up, moving the pieces here and there, playing against himself."

"Wise?"

"Dr. Hasselbacher has got into strange company."

"I know nothing about that."

"Why did you send him a postcard from Santiago marked with the position of your room?"

"What a lot of unimportant things you know, Captain Segura."

"I have a reason to be interested in you, Mr. Wormold. I don't want to see you involved. What was it that Dr.

Hasselbacher wished to tell you tonight? His telephone, you understand, is tapped."

"He wanted to play us a record of *Tristan*."

"And perhaps to speak of this?" Captain Segura reversed a photograph on his desk—a flashlight picture with the characteristic glare of white faces gathered round a heap of smashed metal which had once been a car. "And this?" A young man's face unflinching in the flashlight: an empty cigarette-carton crumpled like his life: a man's foot touching his shoulders.

"Do you know him?"

"No."

Captain Segura depressed a lever and a voice spoke in English from a box on his desk. "Hullo. Hullo, Hasselbacher speaking."

"Is anyone with you, H-Hasselbacher?"

"Yes. Friends."

"What friends?"

"If you must know, Mr. Wormold is here."

"Tell him Raul's dead."

"Dead? But they promised . . ."

"You can't always control an accident, H-Hasselbacher." The voice had a slight hesitation before the aspirate.

"They gave me their word . . ."

"The car turned over too many times."

"They said it would be just a warning."

"It is still a warning. Go in and tell h-him that Raul is dead."

The hiss of the tape went on a moment; a door closed.

"Do you still say you know nothing of Raul?" Segura asked.

Wormold looked at Beatrice. She made a slight negative motion of her head. Wormold said, "I give you my word of honour, Segura, that I didn't even know he existed until tonight."

Segura moved a piece. "Your word of honour?"

"My word of honour."

"You are Milly's father. I have to accept it. But stay

away from naked women and the professor's wife. Good night, Mr. Wormold."

"Good night."

They had reached the door when Segura spoke again. "And our game of checkers, Mr. Wormold. We won't forget that."

The old Hillman was waiting in the street. Wormold said, "I'll leave you with Milly."

"Aren't you going home?"

"It's too late to sleep now."

"Where are you going? Can't I come with you?"

"I want you to stay with Milly in case of accidents. Did you see that photograph?"

"Yes."

They didn't speak again before Lamparilla. Then Beatrice said, "I wish you hadn't given your word of honour. You needn't have gone as far as that."

"No?"

"Oh, it was professional of you, I can see that. I'm sorry. It's stupid of me. But you are more professional than I ever believed you were." He opened the street-door for her and watched her move away among the vacuum cleaners like a mourner in a cemetery.

[2]

At the door of Dr. Hasselbacher's apartment house he rang the bell of a stranger on the second floor whose light was on. There was a buzz and the door unlatched. The lift stood ready and he took it up to Dr. Hasselbacher's flat. Dr. Hasselbacher too had apparently not found sleep. A light shone under the crack of the door. Was he alone or was he in conference with the taped voice?

He was beginning to learn the caution and tricks of his unreal trade. There was a tall window on the landing which led to a purposeless balcony too narrow for use. From this balcony he could see a light in the doctor's flat and it was only a long stride from one balcony to another. He took it without looking at the ground below. The curtains were not quite drawn. He peered between.

Dr. Hasselbacher sat facing him wearing an old *pickelhaube* helmet, a breastplate, boots, white gloves, what could only be the ancient uniform of a Uhlan. His eyes were closed and he seemed to be asleep. He was wearing a sword, and he looked like an extra in a film-studio. Wormold tapped on the window. Dr. Hasselbacher opened his eyes and stared straight at him.

"Hasselbacher."

The doctor gave a small movement that might have been panic. He tried to whip off his helmet, but the chin-strap prevented him.

"It's me, Wormold."

The doctor came reluctantly forward to the window. His breeches were far too tight. They had been made for a younger man.

"What are you doing there, Mr. Wormold?"

"What are you doing there, Hasselbacher?"

The doctor opened the window and let Wormold in. He found that he was in the doctor's bedroom. A big wardrobe stood open and two white suits hung there like the last teeth in an old mouth. Hasselbacher began to take off his gloves. "Have you been to a fancy-dress dance, Hasselbacher?"

Dr. Hasselbacher said in a shamed voice, "You wouldn't understand." He began piece by piece to rid himself of his paraphernalia—first the gloves, then the helmet, the breastplate, in which Wormold and the furnishings of the room were reflected and distorted like figures in a hall of mirrors. "Why did you come back? Why didn't you ring the bell?"

"I want to know who Raul is."

"You know already."

"I've no idea."

Dr. Hasselbacher sat down and pulled at his boots.

"Are you an admirer of Charles Lamb, Dr. Hasselbacher?"

"Milly lent it me. Don't you remember how she talked

of it . . . ?" He sat forlornly in the bulging breeches.
Wormold saw that they had been unstitched along a seam
to allow room for the contemporary Hasselbacher. Yes,
he remembered now the evening at the Tropicana.

"I suppose," Hasselbacher said, "this uniform seems to
you to need an explanation."

"Other things need one more."

"I was a Uhlan officer—oh, forty-five years ago."

"I remember a photograph of you in the other room.
You were not dressed like that. You looked more—
practical."

"That was after the war started. Look over there by my
dressing-table—1913, the June manœuvres, the Kaiser
was inspecting us." The old brown photograph with the
photographer's indented seal in the corner showed the
long ranks of the cavalry, swords drawn, and a little
Imperial figure with a withered arm on a white horse
riding by. "It was all so peaceful," Dr. Hasselbacher said,
"in those days."

"Peaceful?"

"Until the war came."

"But I thought you were a doctor."

"I became one later. When the war was over. After I'd
killed a man. You kill a man—that is so easy," Dr.
Hasselbacher said, "it needs no skill. You can be certain
of what you've done, you can judge death, but to save a
man—that takes more than six years of training, and in
the end you can never be quite sure that it was you who
saved him. Germs are killed by other germs. People just
survive. There is not one patient whom I know for certain
that I saved, but the man I killed—I know him. He was
Russian and he was very thin. I scraped the bone when I
pushed the steel in. It set my teeth on edge. There was
nothing but marshes around, and they called it Tannen-
berg. I hate war, Mr. Wormold."

"Then why do you dress up like a soldier?"

"I was not dressed up in this way when I killed a man.
This was peaceful. I love this." He touched the breastplate beside him on the bed. "But there we had the mud
of the marshes on us." He said, "Do you never have a

desire, Mr. Wormold, to go back to peace? Oh no, I forget, you're young, you've never known it. This was the last peace for any of us. The trousers don't fit any more."

"What made you—tonight—want to dress up like this, Hasselbacher?"

"A man's death."

"Raul?"

"Yes."

"Did you know him?"

"Yes."

"Tell me about him."

"I don't want to talk."

"It would be better to talk."

"We were both responsible for his death, you and I," Hasselbacher said. "I don't know who trapped you into it or how, but if I had refused to help them they would have had me deported. What could I do out of Cuba now? I told you I had lost papers."

"What papers?"

"Never mind that. Don't we all have something in the past to worry about? I know why they broke up my flat now. Because I was a friend of yours. Please go away, Mr. Wormold. Who knows what they might expect me to do if they knew you were here?"

"Who are they?"

"You know that better than I do, Mr. Wormold. They don't introduce themselves." Something moved rapidly in the next room.

"Only a mouse, Mr. Wormold. I keep a little cheese for it at night."

"So Milly lent you Lamb's *Tales*."

"I'm glad you have changed your code," Dr. Hasselbacher said. "Perhaps now they will leave me alone. I can't help them any longer. One begins with acrostics and crosswords and mathematical puzzles and then, before you know, you are employed . . . Nowadays we have to be careful even of our hobbies."

"But Raul—he didn't even exist. You advised me to lie

and I lied. They were nothing but inventions, Hasselbacher."

"And Cifuentes? Are you telling me he didn't exist either?"

"He was different. I invented Raul."

"Then you invented him too well, Mr. Wormold. There's a whole file on him now."

"He was no more real than a character in a novel."

"Are they always invented? I don't know how a novelist works, Mr. Wormold. I have never known one before you."

"There was no drunk pilot in the Cubana air line."

"Oh, I agree, you must have invented that detail. I don't know why."

"If you were breaking my cables you must have realized there was no truth in them, you know the city. A pilot dismissed for drunkenness, a friend with a plane, they were all inventions."

"I don't know your motive, Mr. Wormold. Perhaps you wanted to disguise his identity in case we broke your code. Perhaps if your friends had known he had private means and a plane of his own, they wouldn't have paid him so much. How much of it all got into his pocket, I wonder, and how much into yours?"

"I don't understand a word you're saying."

"You read the papers, Mr. Wormold. You know he had his flying-licence taken away a month ago when he landed drunk in a child's playground."

"I don't read the local papers."

"Never? Of course he denied working for you. They offered him a lot of money if he would work for them instead. They too want photographs, Mr. Wormold, of those platforms you discovered in the Oriente hills."

"There are no platforms."

"Don't expect me to believe too much, Mr. Wormold. You referred in one cable to plans you had sent to London. They needed photographs too."

"You must know who They are."

"Cui bono?"

"And what do they plan for me?"

"At first they promised me they were planning nothing. You have been useful to them. They knew about you from the very beginning, Mr. Wormold, but they didn't take you seriously. They even thought you might be inventing your reports. But then you changed your codes and your staff increased. The British Secret Service would not be so easily deceived as all that, would it?" A kind of loyalty to Hawthorne kept Wormold silent. "Mr. Wormold, Mr. Wormold, why did you ever begin?"

"You know why. I needed the money." He found himself taking to truth like a tranquilliser.

"I would have lent you money. I offered to."

"I needed more than you could lend me."

"For Milly?"

"Yes."

"Take good care of her, Mr. Wormold. You are in a trade where it is unsafe to love anybody or anything. They strike at that. You remember the culture I was making?"

"Yes."

"Perhaps if they hadn't destroyed my will to live, they wouldn't have persuaded me so easily."

"Do you really think . . . ?"

"I only ask you to be careful."

"Can I use your telephone?"

"Yes."

Wormold rang up his house. Did he only imagine that slight click which indicated that the tapper was at work? Beatrice answered. He said, "Is everything quiet?"

"Yes."

"Wait till I come. Is Milly all right?"

"Fast asleep."

"I'm coming back."

Dr. Hasselbacher said, "You shouldn't have shown love in your voice. Who knows who was listening?" He walked with difficulty to the door because of his tight breeches. "Good night, Mr. Wormold. Here is the Lamb."

"I won't need it any more."

"Milly may want it. Would you mind saying nothing to

anyone about this—this—costume? I know that I am absurd, but I loved those days. Once the Kaiser spoke to me."

"What did he say?"

"He said, 'I remember you. You are Captain Müller.'"

Interlude in London

When the Chief had guests he dined at home and cooked his own dinner, for no restaurant satisfied his meticulous and romantic standard. There was a story that once when he was ill he refused to cancel an invitation to an old friend, but cooked the meal from his bed by telephone. With a watch before him on the bed-table he would interrupt the conversation at the correct interval, to give directions to his valet. "Hallo, hallo, Brewer, hallo, you should take that chicken out now and baste it again."

It was also said that once when he had been kept late at the office and had tried to cook the meal from there, dinner had been ruined because from force of habit he had used his red telephone, the scrambler, and only strange noises resembling rapid Japanese had reached the valet's ears.

The meal which he served to the Permanent Under-Secretary was simple and excellent: a roast with a touch of garlic. A Wensleydale cheese stood on the sideboard and the quiet of Albany lay deeply around them like snow. After his exertions in the kitchen the Chief himself smelt faintly of gravy.

"It's really excellent. Excellent."

"An old Norfolk recipe. Granny Brown's Ipswich Roast."

"And the meat itself . . . it really melts . . ."

"I've trained Brewer to do the marketing, but he'll never make a cook. He needs constant supervision."

They ate for a while reverently in silence; the clink of a woman's shoes along the Rope Walk was the only distraction.

"A good wine," the Permanent Under-Secretary said at last.

"'55 is coming along nicely. Still a little young?"

"Hardly."

With the cheese the Chief spoke again. "The Russian note—what does the F.O. think?"

"We are a little puzzled by the reference to the Caribbean bases." There was a crackling of Romary biscuits. "They can hardly refer to the Bahamas. They are worth about what the Yankees paid us, a few old destroyers. Yet we've always assumed that those constructions in Cuba had a Communist origin. You don't think they could have an American origin after all?"

"Wouldn't we have been informed?"

"Not necessarily, I'm afraid. Since the Fuchs case. They say we keep a good deal under our own hat too. What does your man in Havana say?"

"I'll ask him for a full assessment. How's the Wensleydale?"

"Perfect."

"Help yourself to the port."

"Cockburn '35, isn't it?"

"'27."

"Do you believe they intend war eventually?" the Chief asked.

"Your guess is as good as mine."

"They've become very active in Cuba—apparently with the help of the police. Our man in Havana has had a difficult time. His best agent, as you know, was killed, accidentally of course, on his way to take aerial photographs of the constructions—a very great loss to us. But I would give much more than a man's life for those photographs. As it was, we had given fifteen hundred dollars. They shot at another of our agents in the street and he's taken fright. A third's gone underground. There's a woman too, they interrogated her, in spite of her being the mistress of the Director of Posts and Telegraphs. They have left our man alone so far, perhaps to watch. Anyway he's a canny bird."

"Surely he must have been a bit careless to lose all those agents?"

"At the beginning we have to expect casualties. They broke his book-code. I'm never happy with these book-codes. There's a German out there who seems to be their biggest operator and an expert at cryptography. Hawthorne warned our man, but you know what these old merchants are like; they have an obstinate loyalty. Perhaps it was worth a few casualties to open his eyes. Cigar?"

"Thanks. Will he be able to start again if he's blown?"

"He has a trick worth two of that. Struck right home into the enemy-camp. Recruited a double agent in the police-headquarters itself."

"Aren't double agents always a bit—tricky? You never know whether you're getting the fat or the lean."

"I trust our man to huff him every time," the Chief said. "I say huff because they are both great draughts players. Checkers they call it there. As a matter of fact, that's their excuse for contacting each other."

"I can't exaggerate how worried we are about the constructions, C. If only you had got the photographs before they killed your man. The P.M. is pressing us to inform the Yankees and ask their help."

"You mustn't let him. You can't depend on their security."

PART V

[1]

"Huff," said Captain Segura. They had met at the Havana Club. At the Havana Club, which was not a club at all and was owned by Baccardi's rival, all rum-drinks were free, and this enabled Wormold to increase his savings for naturally he continued to charge for the drinks in his expenses—the fact that the drinks were free would have been tedious, if not impossible, to explain to London. The bar was on the first floor of a seventeenth-century house and the windows faced the Cathedral where the body of Christopher Columbus had once lain. A grey stone statue of Columbus stood outside the Cathedral and looked as though it had been formed through the centuries under water, like a coral reef, by the action of insects.

"You know," Captain Segura said, "there was a time when I thought you didn't like me."

"There are other motives for playing draughts than liking a man."

"Yes, for me too," Captain Segura said. "Look! I make a king."

"And I huff you three times."

"You think I did not see that, but you will find the move is in my favour. There, now I take your only king. Why did you go to Santiago, Santa Clara and Cienfuegos two weeks ago?"

"I always go about this time to see the retailers."

"It really looked as though that *was* your reason. You stayed in the new hotel at Cienfuegos. You had dinner alone in a restaurant on the waterfront. You went to a cinema and you went home. Next morning . . ."

"Do you really believe I'm a secret agent?"

"I'm beginning to doubt it. I think our friends have made a mistake."

"Who are our friends?"

"Oh, let's say the friends of Dr. Hasselbacher."

"And who are they?"

"It's my job to know what goes on in Havana," said Captain Segura, "not to take sides or to give information." He was moving his king unchecked up the board.

"Is there anything in Cuba important enough to interest a Secret Service?"

"Of course we are only a small country, but we lie very close to the American coast. And we point at your own Jamaica base. If a country is surrounded, as Russia is, it will try to punch a hole through from inside."

"What use would I be—or Dr. Hasselbacher—in global strategy? A man who sells vacuum cleaners. A retired doctor."

"There are unimportant pieces in any game," said Captain Segura. "Like this one here. I take it and you don't mind losing it. Dr. Hasselbacher, of course, is very good at crosswords."

"What have crosswords to do with it?"

"A man like that makes a good cryptographer. Somebody once showed me a cable of yours with its interpretation, or rather they let me discover it. Perhaps they thought I would run you out of Cuba." He laughed. "Milly's father. They little knew."

"What was it about?"

"You claimed to have recruited Engineer Cifuentes. Of course that was absurd. I know him well. Perhaps they shot at him to make the cable sound more convincing. Perhaps they wrote it because they wanted to get rid of you. Or perhaps they are more credulous than I am."

"What an extraordinary story." He moved a piece. "How are you so certain that Cifuentes is not my agent?"

"By the way you play checkers, Mr. Wormold, and because I interrogated Cifuentes."

"Did you torture him?"

Captain Segura laughed. "No. He doesn't belong to the torturable class."

"I didn't know there were class-distinctions in torture."

"Dear Mr. Wormold, surely you realise there are people who expect to be tortured and others who would be outraged by the idea. One never tortures except by a kind of mutual agreement."

"There's torture and torture. When they broke up Dr. Hasselbacher's laboratory they were torturing . . . ?"

"One can never tell what amateurs may do. The police had no concern in that. Dr. Hasselbacher does not belong to the torturable class."

"Who does?"

"The poor in my own country, in any Latin American country. The poor of Central Europe and the Orient. Of course in your welfare states you have no poor, so you are untorturable. In Cuba the police can deal as harshly as they like with émigrés from Latin America and the Baltic States, but not with visitors from your country or Scandinavia. It is an instinctive matter on both sides. Catholics are more torturable than Protestants, just as they are more criminal. You see, I was right to make that king, and now I shall huff you for the last time."

"You always win, don't you? That's an interesting theory of yours."

"One reason why the West hates the great Communist states is that they don't recognise class-distinctions. Sometimes they torture the wrong people. So too of course did Hitler and shocked the world. Nobody cares what goes on in our prisons, or the prisons of Lisbon or Caracas, but Hitler was too promiscuous. It was rather as though in your country a chauffeur had slept with a peeress."

"We're not shocked by that any longer."

"It is a great danger for everyone when what is shocking changes."

They had another free daiquiri each, frozen so stiffly that it had to be drunk in tiny drops to avoid a sinus-pain. "And how is Milly?" Captain Segura asked.

"Well."

"I'm very fond of the child. She has been properly brought up."

"I'm glad you think so."

"That is another reason why I would not wish you to get into any trouble, Mr. Wormold, which might mean the loss of your residence-permit. Havana would be poorer without your daughter."

"I don't suppose you really believe me, Captain, but Cifuentes was no agent of mine."

"I do believe you. I think perhaps someone wanted to use you as a stalking-horse, or perhaps as one of those painted ducks which attract the real wild ducks to settle." He finished his daiquiri. "That of course suits my book. I too like to watch the wild duck come in, from Russia, America, England, even Germany once again. They despise the poor local dago marksman, but one day, when they are all settled, what a shoot I will have."

"It's a complicated world. I find it easier to sell vacuum cleaners."

"The business prospers, I hope?"

"Oh yes, yes."

"I was interested that you had enlarged your staff. That charming secretary with the siphon and the coat that wouldn't close. And the young man."

"I need someone to superintend accounts. Lopez is not reliable."

"Ah, Lopez. Another of your agents." Captain Segura laughed. "Or so it was reported to me."

"Yes. He supplies me with secret information about the police-department."

"Be careful, Mr. Wormold. He is one of the torturable." They both laughed, drinking daiquiries. It is easy to laugh at the idea of torture on a sunny day. "I must be going, Mr. Wormold."

"I suppose the cells are full of my spies."

"We can always make room for another by having a few executions."

"One day, Captain, I am going to beat you at draughts."

"I doubt it, Mr. Wormold."

From the window he watched Captain Segura pass the grey pumice-like figure of Columbus on the way to his office. Then he had another free daiquiri. The Havana Club and Captain Segura seemed to have taken the place of the Wonder Bar and Dr. Hasselbacher—it was like a change of life and he had to make the best of it. There was no turning time back. Dr. Hasselbacher had been humiliated in front of him, and friendship cannot stand humiliation. He had not seen Dr. Hasselbacher again. In the club he felt himself, as in the Wonder Bar, a citizen of Havana; the elegant young man who brought him a drink made no attempt to sell him one of the assorted bottles of rum arranged on his table. A man with a grey beard read his morning paper as always at this hour; as usual a postman had interrupted his daily round for his free drink: all of them were citizens too. Four tourists left the bar carrying woven baskets, containing bottles of rum; they were flushed and cheerful and harboured the illusion that their drinks had cost them nothing. He thought, They are the foreigners, and of course untorturable.

Wormold drank his daiquiri too fast and left the Havana Club with his eyes aching. The tourists leant over the seventeenth-century well; they had flung into it enough coins to have paid for their drinks twice over: they were ensuring a happy return. A woman's voice called him and he saw Beatrice standing between the pillars of the colonnade among the gourds and rattles and Negro-dolls of the curio-shop.

"What are you doing here?"

She explained, "I'm always unhappy when you meet Segura. This time I wanted to be sure . . ."

"Sure of what?" He wondered whether at last she had begun to suspect that he had no agents. Perhaps she had received instructions to watch him, from London or from 59200 in Kingston. They began to walk home.

"Sure that it's not a trap, that the police aren't waiting for you. A double agent is tricky to handle."

"You worry too much."

"And you have so little experience. Look what happened to Raul and Cifuentes."

"Cifuentes has been interrogated by the police." He added with relief, "He's blown, so he's no use to us now."

"Then aren't you blown too?"

"He gave nothing away. It was Captain Segura who chose the questions, and Segura is one of us. I think perhaps it's time we gave him a bonus. He's trying to compile a complete list for us of foreign agents here— American as well as Russian. Wild duck—that's what he calls them."

"It would be quite a coup. And the constructions?"

"We'll have to let those rest a while. I can't make him act against his own country."

Passing the Cathedral he gave his usual coin to the blind beggar who sat on the steps outside. Beatrice said, "It seems almost worth while being blind in this sun." The creative instinct stirred in Wormold. He said, "You know, he's not really blind. He sees everything that goes on."

"He must be a good actor. I've been watching him all the time you were with Segura."

"And he's been watching you. As a matter of fact he's one of my best informers. I always have him stationed here when I meet Segura. An elementary precaution. I'm not as careless as you think."

"You've never told H.Q."

"There's no point. They could hardly have traces of a blind beggar, and I don't use him for information. All the same if I had been arrested you'd have known of it in ten minutes. What would you have done?"

"Burnt all records and driven Milly to the Embassy."

"What about Rudy?"

"I'd have told him to radio London that we were breaking off and then to go underground."

"How does one go underground?" He didn't probe for an answer. He said slowly as the story grew of itself, "The beggar's name is Miguel. He really does all this for love. You see, I saved his life once."

"How?"

"Oh, it was nothing. An accident to the ferry. It just happened that I could swim and he couldn't."

"Did they give you a medal?" He looked at her quickly, but in her face he could see only innocent interest.

"No. There was no glory. As a matter of fact they fined me for bringing him to shore in a defence zone."

"What a very romantic story. And now of course he would give his life for you."

"Oh, I wouldn't go as far as that."

"Do tell me—have you somewhere a small penny account-book in black wash-leather?"

"I shouldn't think so. Why?"

"With your first purchases of pen-nibs and india-rubbers?"

"Why on earth pen-nibs?"

"I was just wondering, that's all."

"You can't buy account-books for a penny. And pen-nibs—nobody uses pen-nibs nowadays."

"Forget it. Just something Henry said to me. A natural mistake."

"Who's Henry?" he asked.

"59200," she said. He felt an odd jealousy, for in spite of security rules she had only once called him Jim.

The house was empty as usual when they came in; he was aware that he no longer missed Milly, and he felt the sad relief of a man who realises that there is one love at least that no longer hurts him.

"Rudy's out," Beatrice said. "Buying sweets, I suppose. He eats too many. He must consume an awful lot of energy, because he gets no fatter, but I don't see how."

"We'd better get down to work. There's a cable to send. Segura gave some valuable information about Communist infiltration in the police. You'd hardly believe . . ."

"I can believe almost anything. Look at this. I've just discovered something fascinating in the code-book. Did you know there was a group for 'eunuch'? Do you think it crops up often in cables?"

"I expect they need it in the Istanbul office."

"I wish we could use it. Can't we?"

"Are you ever going to marry again?"

Beatrice said, "Your free associations are rather obvious sometimes. Do you think Rudy has a secret life? He can't consume all that energy in the office."

"What's the drill for a secret life? Do you have to ask permission from London before you start one?"

"Well, of course, you would have to get traces before going very far. London prefers to keep sex inside the department."

[2]

i

"I must be getting important," Wormold said. "I've been invited to make a speech."

"Where?" Milly asked, looking politely up from the *Horsewoman's Year Book*. It was the evening hour when work was over and the last gold light lay flat across the roofs and touched the honey-coloured hair and the whisky in his glass.

"At the annual lunch of the European Traders' Association. Dr. Braun, the President, has asked me to make one—as the oldest member. The guest of honour is the American Consul-General," he added with pride. It seemed such a short time ago that he had come to Havana and met with her family in the Floridita bar the girl who was Milly's mother; now he was the oldest trader there. Many had retired: some had gone home to fight in the last war—English, German, French—but he had been rejected because of his bad leg. None of these had returned to Cuba.

"What will you talk about?"

He said sadly, "I shan't. I wouldn't know what to say."

"I bet you'd speak better than any of them."

"Oh no. I may be the oldest member, Milly, but I'm the smallest too. The rum-exporters and the cigar-men—they are the really important people."

"You are you."

"I wish you had chosen a cleverer father."

"Captain Segura says you are pretty good at checkers."

"But not as good as he is."

"Please accept, Father," she said. "I'd be so proud of you."

"I'd make a fool of myself."

"You wouldn't. For my sake."

"For your sake I'd turn cartwheels. All right. I'll accept."

Rudy knocked at the door. This was the hour when he listened in for the last time; it would be midnight in London. He said, "There's an urgent cable from Kingston. Shall I fetch Beatrice?"

"No, I can manage it myself. She's going to a movie."

"Business does seem brisk," Milly said.

"Yes."

"But you don't seem to *sell* any more cleaners."

"It's all long-term promotion," Wormold said.

He went into his bedroom and deciphered the cable. It was from Hawthorne. Wormold was to come by the first possible plane to Kingston and report. He thought: So they know at last.

ii

The rendezvous was the Myrtle Bank Hotel. Wormold had not been to Jamaica for many years, and he was appalled by the dirt and the heat. What accounted for the squalor of British possessions? The Spanish, the French and the Portuguese built cities where they settled, but the English just allowed cities to grow. The poorest street in Havana had dignity compared with the shanty-life of Kingston—huts built out of old petrol-tins roofed with scrap-metal purloined from some cemetery of abandoned cars.

Hawthorne sat in a long chair in the veranda of Myrtle Bank drinking a planter's punch through a straw. His suit was just as immaculate as when Wormold had met him first; the only sign of the great heat was a little powder caked under his left ear. He said, "Take a pew." Even the slang was back.

"Thanks."

"Had a good trip?"

"Yes, thank you."

"I expect you're glad to be at home."

"Home?"

"I mean here—having a holiday from the dagoes. Back in British territory." Wormold thought of the huts he had seen along the harbour and a hopeless old man asleep in a patch of shade and a ragged child nursing a piece of driftwood. He said, "Havana's not so bad."

"Have a planter's punch. They are good here."

"Thanks."

Hawthorne said, "I asked you to come over because there's a spot of trouble."

"Yes?" He supposed that the truth was coming out. Could he be arrested now that he was on British territory? What would the charge be? Obtaining money on false pretences perhaps or some obscurer charge heard *in camera* under the Official Secrets Act.

"About these constructions."

He wanted to explain that Beatrice knew nothing of all this; he had no accomplice except the credulity of other men.

"What about them?" he asked.

"I wish you'd been able to get photographs."

"I tried. You know what happened."

"Yes. The drawings are a bit confusing."

"They are not by a skilled draughtsman."

"Don't get me wrong, old man. You've done wonders, but, you know, there was a time when I was—almost suspicious."

"What of?"

"Well, some of them sort of reminded me—to be frank, they reminded me of parts of a vacuum cleaner."

"Yes, that struck me too."

"And then, you see, I remembered all the thingummies in your shop."

"You thought I'd pulled the leg of the Secret Service?"

"Of course it sounds fantastic now, I know. All the same, in a way I was relieved when I found that the others have made up their minds to murder you."

"Murder me?"

"You see, that really proves the drawings are genuine."

"What others?"

"The other side. Of course I'd luckily kept these absurd suspicions to myself."

"How are they going to murder me?"

"Oh, we'll come to that—a matter of poisoning. What I mean is that next to having photographs one can't have a better confirmation of your reports. We had been rather sitting on them, but we've circulated them now to all the Service Departments. We sent them to Atomic Research as well. They weren't helpful. Said they had no connexion with nuclear fission. The trouble is we've been bemused by the atom-boys and have quite forgotten that there may be other forms of scientific warfare just as dangerous."

"How are they going to poison me?"

"First things first, old man. One mustn't forget the economics of warfare. Cuba can't afford to start making H-bombs, but have they found something equally effective at short range and *cheap?* That's the important word —cheap."

"Please would you mind telling me how they are going to murder me? You see, it interests me personally."

"Of course I'm going to tell you. I just wanted to give you the background first and to tell you how pleased we all are—at the confirmation of your reports, I mean. They plan to poison you at some sort of business lunch."

"The European Traders' Association?"

"I think that's the name."

"How do you know?"

"We've penetrated their oganisation here. You'd be surprised how much we know of what goes on in your territory. I can tell you for instance that the death of stroke four was an accident. They just wanted to scare

him as they scared stroke three by shooting at him. You
are the first one they've really decided to murder."

"That's comforting."

"In a way, you know, it's a compliment. You are
dangerous now." Hawthorne made a long sucking noise,
draining up the last liquid between the layers of ice and
orange and pineapple and the cherry on top.

"I suppose," Wormold said, "I'd better not go." He felt
a surprising disappointment. "It will be the first lunch I've
missed in ten years. They'd even asked me to speak. The
firm always expects me to attend. Like showing the
flag."

"But of *course* you've got to go."

"And be poisoned?"

"You needn't eat anything, need you?"

"Have you ever tried going to a public lunch and not
eating anything? There's also the question of drink."

"They can't very well poison a bottle of wine. You
could give the impression of being an alcoholic, somebody
who doesn't eat but only drinks."

"Thank you. That would certainly be good for business."

"People have a soft spot in their hearts for alcoholics,"
Hawthorne said. "Besides, if you don't go they'll suspect
something. It puts my source in danger. We have to
protect our sources."

"That's the drill I suppose."

"Exactly, old man. Another point: We know the plot,
but we don't know the plotters, except their symbols. If
we discover who they are, we can insist on having them
locked up. We'll disrupt the organisation."

"Yes, there aren't any perfect murders, are there? I
dare say there'll be a clue at the post-mortem on which
you can persuade Segura to act."

"You aren't afraid, are you? This is a dangerous job.
You shouldn't have taken it unless you were prepared . . ."

"You're like a Spartan mother, Hawthorne. Come back
victorious or stay beneath the table."

"That's quite an idea, you know. You could slip under
the table at the right moment. The murderers would think

you were dead and the others would just think you were drunk."

"This is not a meeting of the Big Four at Moscow. The European Traders don't fall under the table."

"Never?"

"Never. You think I'm unduly concerned, don't you?"

"I don't think there's any need for you to worry yet. They don't serve you, after all. You help yourself."

"Of course. Except that there's always a Morro crab to start with at the Nacional. That's prepared in advance."

"You mustn't eat that. Lots of people don't eat crab. When they serve the other courses never take the portion next to you. It's like a conjuror forcing a card on you. You just have to reject it."

"But the conjuror usually manages to force the card just the same."

"I tell you what—did you say the lunch was at the Nacional?"

"Yes."

"Then why can't you use stroke seven?"

"Who's stroke seven?"

"Don't you remember your own agents? Surely he's the head waiter at the Nacional? He can help to see your plate isn't tampered with. It's time he did something for his money. I don't remember you sending a single report from him."

"Can't you give me any idea who the man at the lunch will be? I mean the man who plans to . . ." he boggled at the word "kill" . . . "to do it."

"Not a clue, old man. Just be careful of everyone. Have another planter's punch."

iii

The plane back to Cuba had few passengers: a Spanish woman with a pack of children—some of them screamed and some of them were air-sick as soon as they left the ground; a negress with a live cock wrapped in her shawl; a Cuban cigar-exporter with whom Wormold had a nodding acquaintance, and an Englishman in a tweed jacket who smoked a pipe until the air-hostess told him to put it out. Then he sucked the empty pipe ostentatiously for the rest of the journey and sweated heavily into the tweed. He had the ill-humoured face of a man who is always in the right.

When lunch was served he moved back several places and sat down beside Wormold. He said, "Can't stand those screaming brats. Do you mind?" He looked at the papers on Wormold's knee. "You with Phastkleaners?" he said.

"Yes."

"I'm with Nucleaners. The name's Carter."

"Oh."

"This is only my second trip to Cuba. Gay spot, they tell me," he said, blowing down his pipe and laying it aside for lunch.

"It can be," Wormold said, "if you like roulette or brothels."

Carter patted his tobacco-pouch as though it were a dog's head—"my faithful hound shall bear me company." "I didn't exactly mean . . . though I'm not a Puritan, mind. I suppose it would be interesting. Do as the Romans do." He changed the subject. "Sell many of your machines?"

"Trade's not so bad."

"We've got a new model that's gong to wipe the market." He took a large mouthful of sweet mauve cake and then cut himself a piece of chicken.

"Really."

"Runs on a motor like a lawn-mower. No effort by the little woman. No tubes trailing all over the place."

"Noisy?"

"Special silencer. Less noise than your model. We are calling it the Whisper-Wife." After taking a swig of turtle soup he began to eat his fruit salad, crunching the grape stones between his teeth. He said, "We are opening an agency in Cuba soon. Know Dr. Braun?"

"I've met him. At the European Traders' Association.

He's our President. Imports precision-instruments from Geneva."

"That's the man. He's given us very useful advice. In fact I'm going to your bean-feast as his guest. Do they give you a good lunch?"

"You know what hotel-lunches are like."

"Better than this anyway." he said, spitting out a grape-skin. He had overlooked the asparagus in mayonnaise and now began on that. Afterwards he fumbled in his pocket. "Here's my card." The card read: "William Carter B. Tech. (Nottwich)" and in the corner, "Nucleaners Ltd." He said, "I'm staying at the Seville-Biltmore for a week."

"I'm afraid I haven't a card on me. My name's Wormold."

"Met a fellow called Davis?"

"I don't think so."

"Shared digs with him at college. He went into Gripfix and came out to this part of the world. It's funny—you find Nottwich men everywhere. You weren't there yourself, were you?"

"No."

"Reading?"

"I wasn't at a University."

"I couldn't have told it," Carter told him kindly. "I'd have gone to Oxford, you know, but they are very backward in technology. All right for schoolmasters, I suppose." He began to suck again at his empty pipe like a child at a comforter, till it whistled between his teeth. Suddenly he spoke again, as though some remains of tannin had touched his tongue with a bitter flavour. "Outdated," he said, "relics, living on the past. I'd abolish them."

"Abolish what?"

"Oxford and Cambridge." He took the only food that was left in the tray, a roll of bread, and crumbled it like age or ivy crumbling a stone.

At the Customs Wormold lost him. He was having trouble with his sample Nucleaner, and Wormold saw no reason why the representative of Phastkleaners should

assist him to enter. Beatrice was there to meet him wit
the Hillman. It was many years since he had been met b
a woman.

"Everything all right?" she asked.

"Yes. Oh yes. They seem pleased with me." He watche
her hands on the wheel; she wore no gloves in the ho
afternoon; they were beautiful and competent hands. H
said, "You aren't wearing your ring."

She said, "I didn't think anyone would notice. Milly di
too. You are an observant family."

"You haven't lost it?"

"I took it off yesterday to wash and I forgot to put i
back. There's no point, is there, wearing a ring you for
get?"

It was then he told her about the lunch.

"You won't go?" she said.

"Hawthorne expects me to. To protect his source."

"Damn his source."

"There's a better reason. Something that Dr. Hassel
bacher said to me. They like to strike at what you love. I
I don't go, they'll think up something else. Somethin
worse. And we shan't know what. Next time it mightn't b
me—I don't think I love myself enough to satisfy them—
it might be Milly. Or you." He didn't realise the implica
tion of what he had said until she had dropped him at hi
door and driven on.

[3]

i

Milly said, "You've had a cup of coffee, and that's all
Not even a piece of toast."

"I'm just not in the mood."

"You'll go and over-eat at the Traders' lunch today
and you know perfectly well that Morro crab doesn'
agree with your stomach."

"I promise you I'll be very very careful."

"You'd do much better to have a proper breakfast. You need a cereal to mop up all the liquor you'll be drinking." It was one of her duenna days.

"I'm sorry, Milly, I just can't. I've got things on my mind. Please don't pester me. Not today."

"Have you prepared your speech?"

"I've done my best, but I'm no speaker, Milly. I don't know why they asked me." But he was uneasily conscious that perhaps he did know why. Somebody must have brought influence to bear on Dr. Braun, somebody who had to be identified at any cost. He thought, I am the cost.

"I bet you'll be a sensation."

"I'm trying hard not to be a sensation at this lunch."

Milly went to school and he sat on at the table. The cereal company which Milly patronised had printed on the carton of Weatbrix the latest adventure of Little Dwarf Doodoo. Little Dwarf Doodoo in a rather brief instalment encountered a rat the size of a St. Bernard dog and he frightened the rat away by pretending to be a cat and saying miaou. It was a very simple story. You could hardly call it a preparation for life. The company also gave away an air-gun in return for twelve lids. As the packet was almost empty Wormold began to cut off the lid, driving his knife carefully along the dotted line. He was turning the last corner when Beatrice entered. She said, "What are you doing?"

"I thought an air-gun might be useful in the office. We only need eleven more lids."

"I couldn't sleep last night."

"Too much coffee?"

"No. Something you told me Dr. Hasselbacher said. About Milly. Please don't go to the lunch."

"It's the least I can do."

"You do quite enough. They are pleased with you in London. I can tell that from the way they cable you. Whatever Henry may say, London wouldn't want you to run a silly risk."

"It's quite true what he said—that if I don't go they will try something else."

"Don't worry about Milly. I'll watch her like a lynx."

"And who's going to watch you?"

"I'm in this line of business; it's my own choice. You needn't feel responsible for me."

"Have you been in a spot like this before?"

"No, but I've never had a boss like you before. You seem to stir them up. You know, this job is usually just an office desk and files and dull cables; we don't go in for murder. And I don't want you murdered. You see, you are real. You aren't *Boy's Own Paper*. For God's sake put down that silly packet and listen to me."

"I was re-reading Little Dwarf Doodoo."

"Then stay at home with him this morning. I'll go out and buy you all the back cartons so that you can catch up."

"All Hawthorne said was sense. I only have to be careful what I eat. It *is* important to find out who they are. Then I'll have done something for my money."

"You've done plenty as it is. There's no point in going to this damned lunch."

"Yes, there is a point. Pride."

"Who are you showing off to?"

"You."

ii

He made his way through the lounge of the Nacional Hotel between the show-cases full of Italian shoes and Danish ash-trays and Swedish glass and mauve British woollies. The private dining-room where the European Traders always met lay just beyond the chair where Dr. Hasselbacher now sat, conspicuously waiting. Wormold approached with slowing steps; it was the first time he had seen Dr. Hasselbacher since the night when he had sat on the bed in his Uhlan's uniform talking of the past. Members of the Association, passing in to the private dining-room, stopped and spoke to Dr. Hasselbacher; he paid them no attention.

Wormold reached the chair where he sat. Dr. Hasselbacher said, "Don't go in there, Mr. Wormold." He spoke without lowering his voice, the words shivering among the show-cases, attracting attention.

"How are you, Hasselbacher?"

"I said, don't go in."

"I heard you the first time."

"They are going to kill you, Mr. Wormold."

"How do you know that, Hasselbacher?"

"They are planning to poison you in there."

Several of the guests stopped and stared and smiled. One of them, an American, said, "Is the food that bad?" and everyone laughed.

Wormold said, "Don't stay here, Hasselbacher. You are too conspicuous."

"Are you going in?"

"Of course, I'm one of the speakers."

"There's Milly. Don't forget her."

"Don't worry about Milly. I'm going to come out on my feet, Hasselbacher. Please go home."

"All right, but I had to try," Dr. Hasselbacher said. "I'll be waiting at the telephone."

"I'll call you when I leave."

"Good-bye, Jim."

"Good-bye, Doctor." The use of his first name took Wormold unawares. It reminded him of what he had always jokingly thought: that Dr. Hasselbacher would use the name only at his bedside when he had given up hope. He felt suddenly frightened, alone, a long way from home.

"Wormold," a voice said, and turning he saw that it was Carter of Nucleaners, but it was also for Wormold at that moment the English midlands, English snobbery, English vulgarity, all the sense of kinship and security the word England implied to him.

"Carter!" he exclaimed, as though Carter were the one man in Havana he wanted most to meet, and at that instant he was.

"Damned glad to see you," Carter said. "Don't know a soul at this lunch. Not even my—not even Dr. Braun."

His pocket bulged with his pipe and his pouch; he patted them as though for reassurance, as though he too felt far from home.

"Carter, this is Dr. Hasslebacher, an old friend of mine."

"Good day, Doctor." He said to Wormold, "I was looking all over the place for you last night. I don't seem able to find the right spots."

They moved in together to the private dining-room. It was quite irrational, the confidence he had in a fellow-countryman, but on the side where Carter walked he felt protected.

iii

The dining-room had been decorated with two big flags of the United States in honour of the Consul-General, and little paper flags, as in an airport-restaurant, indicated where each national was to sit. There was a Swiss flag at the head of the table for Dr. Braun, the President; there was even the flag of Monaco for the Monegasque Consul who was one of the largest exporters of cigars in Havana. He was to sit on the Consul-General's right hand in recognition of the Royal alliance. Cocktails were circulating when Wormold and Carter entered, and a waiter at once approached them. Was it Wormold's imagination or did the waiter shift the tray so that the last remaining daiquiri lay nearest to Wormold's hand?

"No. No thank you."

Carter put out his hand, but the waiter had already moved on towards the service-door.

"Perhaps you would prefer a dry Martini, sir?" a voice said. He turned. It was the head-waiter.

"No, no, I don't like them."

"A Scotch, sir? A sherry? An Old-Fashioned? Anything you care to order."

"I'm not drinking." Wormold said, and the head-waiter abandoned him for another guest. Presumably he was stroke seven; strange if by an ironic coincidence he was

also the would-be assassin. Wormold looked around for
Carter, but he had moved away in pursuit of his host.

"You'd do better to drink all you can," said a voice
with a Scotch accent. "My name is MacDougall. It seems
we're sitting together."

"I haven't seen you here before, have I?"

"I've taken over from McIntyre. You'd have known
McIntyre surely?"

"Oh yes, yes." Dr. Braun, who had palmed off the
unimportant Carter upon another Swiss who dealt in
watches, was now leading the American Consul-General
round the room, introducing him to the more exclusive
members. The Germans formed a group apart, rather
suitably against the west wall; they carried the superiority
of the deutschmark on their features like duelling scars:
national honour which had survived Belsen depended
now on a rate of exchange. Wormold wondered whether it
was one of them who had betrayed the secret of the lunch
to Dr. Hasselbacher. Betrayed? Not necessarily. Perhaps
the doctor had been blackmailed to supply the poison. At
any rate he would have chosen, for the sake of old
friendship, something painless, if any poison were painless.

"I was telling you," Mr. MacDougall went energetically
on like a Scottish reel, "that you would do better to drink
now. It's all you'll be getting."

"There'll be wine, won't there?"

"Look at the table." Small individual milk-bottles stood
by every place. "Didn't you read your invitation? An
American blue-plate lunch in honour of our great American allies."

"Blue-plate?"

"Surely you know what a blue-plate is, man? They
shove the whole meal at you under your nose, already
dished up on your plate—roast turkey, cranberry sauce,
sausages and carrots and French fried. I can't bear
French fried, but there's no pick and choose with a blue-
plate."

"No pick and choose?"

"You eat what you're given. That's democracy, man."

Dr. Braun was summoning them to the table. Wormold had a hope that fellow-nationals would sit together and that Carter would be on his other side, but it was a strange Scandinavian who sat on his left scowling at his milk-bottle. Wormold thought, Someone has arranged this well. Nothing is safe, not even the milk. Already the waiters were bustling round the board with the Morro crabs. Then he saw with relief that Carter faced him across the table. There was something so secure in his vulgarity. You could appeal to him as you could appeal to an English policeman, because you knew his thoughts.

"No," he said to the waiter, "I won't take crab."

"You are wise not to take those things," Mr. MacDougall said. "I'm refusing them myself. They don't go with whisky. Now if you will drink a little of your iced water and hold it under the table, I've got a flask in my pocket with enough for the two of us."

Without thinking, Wormold stretched out his hand to his glass, and then the doubt came. Who was MacDougall? He had never seen him before, and he hadn't heard until now that McIntyre had gone away. Wasn't it possible that the water was poisoned, or even the whisky in the flask?

"Why did McIntrye leave?" he asked, his hand round the glass.

"Oh, it was just one of those things," Mr. MacDougall said, "you know the way it is. Toss down your water. You don't want to drown the Scotch. This is the best Highland malt."

"It's too early in the day for me. Thank you all the same."

"If you don't trust the water, you are right not to," Mr. MacDougall said ambiguously. "I'm taking it neat myself. If you don't mind sharing the cap of the flask . . ."

"No, really. I don't drink at this hour."

"It was the English who made hours for drinking, not the Scotch. They'll be making hours for dying next."

Carter said across the table, "I don't mind if I do. The

name's Carter," and Wormold saw with relief that Mr. MacDougall was pouring out the whisky; there was one suspicion less, for no one surely would want to poison Carter. All the same, he thought, there is something wrong with Mr. MacDougall's Scottishness. It smelt of fraud like Ossian.

"Svenson," the gloomy Scandinavian said sharply from behind his little Swedish flag; at least Wormold thought it was Swedish: he could never distinguish with certainty between the Scandinavian colours.

"Wormold," he said.

"What is all this nonsense of the milk?"

"I think," Wormold said, "that Dr. Braun is being a little too literal."

"Or funny," Carter said.

"I don't think Dr. Braun has much sense of humour."

"And what do you do, Mr. Wormold?" the Swede asked. "I don't think we have met before, although I know you by sight."

"Vacuum cleaners. And you?"

"Glass. As you know, Swedish glass is the best in the world. This bread is very good. Do you not eat bread?" He might have prepared his conversation beforehand from a phrase-book.

"Given it up. Fattening, you know."

"I would have said you could have done with fattening." Mr. Svenson gave a dreary laugh like jollity in a long northern night. "Forgive me. I make you sound like a goose."

At the end of the table, where the Consul-General sat, they were beginning to serve the blue-plates. Mr. MacDougall had been wrong about the turkey; the main course was Maryland chicken. But he was right about the carrots and the French fried and the sausages. Dr. Braun was a little behind the rest; he was still picking at his Morro crab. The Consul-General must have slowed him down by the earnestness of his conversation and the fixity of his convex lenses. Two waiters came round the table, one whisking away the remains of the crab, the other substituting the blue-plates. Only the Consul-General had thought to open his milk. The word "Dulles" drifted dully down to where Wormold sat. The waiter approached carrying two plates; he put one in front of the Scandinavian, the other was Wormold's. The thought that the whole threat to his life might be a nonsensical practical joke came to Wormold. Perhaps Hawthorne was a humourist, and Dr. Hasselbacher. . . . He remembered Milly asking whether Dr. Hasselbacher ever pulled his leg. Sometimes it seems easier to run the risk of death than ridicule. He wanted to confide in Carter and hear his common-sense reply; then looking at his plate he noticed something odd. There were no carrots. He said quickly, "You prefer it without carrots," and slipped the plate along to Mr. MacDougall.

"It's the French fried I dislike," said Mr. MacDougall quickly and passed the plate on to the Luxemburg Consul. The Luxemburg Consul, who was deep in conversation with a German across the table, handed the plate with absent-minded politeness to his neighbour. Politeness infected all who had not yet been served, and the plate went whisking along towards Dr. Braun, who had just had the remains of his Morro crab removed. The head-waiter saw what was happening and began to stalk the plate up the table, but it kept a pace ahead of him. The waiter, returning with more blue-plates, was intercepted by Wormold, who took one. He looked confused. Wormold began to eat with appetite. "The carrots are excellent," he said.

The head-waiter hovered by Dr. Braun. "Excuse me, Dr. Braun," he said, "they have given you no carrots."

"I don't like carrots," Dr. Braun said, cutting up a piece of chicken.

"I am so sorry," the head-waiter said and seized Dr. Braun's plate. "A mistake in the kitchen." Plate in hand like a verger with the collection he walked up the length of the room towards the service-door. Mr. MacDougall was taking a sip of his own whisky.

"I think I might venture now," Wormold said. "As a celebration."

"Good man. Water or straight?"

"Could I take your water? Mine's got a fly in it."

"Of course." Wormold drank two-thirds of the water and held it out for the whisky from Mr. MacDougall's flask. Mr. MacDougall gave him a generous double. "Hold it out again. You are behind the two of us," he said, and Wormold was back in the territory of trust. He felt a kind of tenderness for the neighbour he had suspected. He said, "We must see each other again."

"An occasion like this would be useless if it didn't bring people together."

"I wouldn't have met you or Carter without it."

They all three had another whisky. "You must both meet my daughter," Wormold said, the whisky warming his cockles.

"How is business with you?"

"Not so bad. We are expanding the office."

Dr. Braun rapped the table for silence.

"Surely," Carter said in the loud irrepressible Nottwich voice as warming as the whisky, "they'll have to serve drinks with the toast."

"My lad," Mr. MacDougall said, "there'll be speeches but no toasts. We have to listen to the bastards without alcoholic aid."

"I'm one of the bastards," Wormold said.

"You speaking?"

"As the oldest member."

"I'm glad you've survived long enough for that," Mr. MacDougall said.

The American Consul-General, called on by Dr. Braun, began to speak. He spoke of the spiritual links between the democracies—he seemed to number Cuba among the democracies. Trade was important because without trade there would be no spiritual links, or was it perhaps the other way round. He spoke of American aid to distressed countries which would enable them to buy more goods and by buying more goods strengthen the spiritual links. . . . A dog was howling somewhere in the wastes of the hotel and the head-waiter signalled for the door to be closed. It had been a great pleasure to the

American Consul-General to be invited to this lunch to-day and to meet the leading representatives of European trade and so strengthen still further the spiritual links. . . . Wormold had two more whiskies.

"And now," Dr. Braun said, "I am going to call upon the oldest member of our Association. I am not of course referring to his years, but to the length of time he has served the cause of European trade in this beautiful city where, Mr. Minister"—he bowed to his other neighbour, a dark man with a squint—"we have the privilege and happiness of being your guests. I am speaking, you all know, of Mr. Wormold." He took a quick look at his notes, "Mr. James Wormold, the Havana representative of Phastkleaners."

Mr. MacDougall said, "We've finished the whisky. Fancy that now. Just when you need your Dutch courage most."

Carter said, "I came armed as well, but I drank most of it in the plane. There's only one glass left in the flask."

"Obviously our friend here must have it," Mr. MacDougall said. "His need is greater than ours."

Dr. Braun said, "We may take Mr. Wormold as a symbol for all that service means—modesty, quietness, perseverance and efficiency. Our enemies picture the salesman often as a loud-mouthed braggart who is intent only on putting across some product which is useless, unnecessary, or even harmful. That is not a true picture . . ."

Wormold said, "It's kind of you, Carter. I could certainly do with a drink."

"Not used to speaking?"

"It's not only the speaking." He leant forward across the table towards that common-or-garden Nottwich face on which he felt he could rely for incredulity, reassurance, the easy humour based on inexperience: he was safe with Carter. He said, "I know you won't believe a word of what I'm telling you," but he didn't want Carter to believe. He wanted to learn from him how not to believe. Something nudged his leg and looking down he

aw a black dachshund-face pleading with him between
he drooping ringlet ears for a scrap—the dog must have
lipped in through the service-door unseen by the waiters
ind now it led a hunted life, half hidden below the
able-cloth.

Carter pushed a small flask across to Wormold.
'There's not enough for two. Take it all."

"Very kind of you, Carter." He unscrewed the top and
oured all that there was into his glass.

"Only a Johnnie Walker. Nothing fancy."

Dr. Braun said, "If anyone here can speak for all of us
bout the long years of patient service a trader gives to
he public, I am sure it is Mr. Wormold, whom now I call
pon . . ."

Carter winked and raised an imaginary glass.

"H-hurry," Carter said. "You've got to h-hurry."

Wormold lowered the whisky. "What did you say, Car-
er?"

"I said drink it up quick."

"Oh no, you didn't, Carter." Why hadn't he noticed
hat stammered aspirate before? Was Carter conscious of
t and did he avoid an initial "h" except when he was
reoccupied by fear or h-hope?

"What's the matter, Wormold?"

Wormold put his hand down to pat the dog's head and
s though by accident he knocked the glass from the
able.

"You pretended not to know the doctor."

"What doctor?"

"You would call him H-Hasselbacher."

"Mr. Wormold," Dr. Braun called down the table.

He rose uncertainly to his feet. The dog for want of any
etter provender was lapping at the whisky on the
oor.

Wormold said, "I appreciate your asking me to speak,
vhatever your motives." A polite titter took him by sur-
rise—he hadn't meant to say anything funny. He said,
This is my first and it looked at one time as though it
vas going to be my last public appearance." He caught
arter's eye. Carter was frowning. He felt guilty of a

solecism by his survival as though he were drunk i
public. Perhaps he was drunk. He said, "I don't kno
whether I've got any friends here. I've certainly got som
enemies." Somebody said "Shame" and several peopl
laughed. If this went on he would get the reputation c
being a witty speaker. He said, "We hear a lot nowaday
about the cold war, but any trader will tell you that th
war between two manufacturers of the same goods can b
quite a hot war. Take Phastkleaners and Nucleaner
There's not much difference between the two machin
any more than there is between two human beings, or
Russian—or German—and one British. There would t
no competition and no war if it wasn't for the ambition c
a few men in both firms; just a few men dictate compet
tion and invent needs and set Mr. Carter and myself
each other's throats."

Nobody laughed now. Dr. Braun whispered somethir
into the ear of the Consul-General. Wormold lifted Ca
ter's whisky-flask and said, "I don't suppose Mr. Cart
even knows the name of the man who sent him to poisc
me for the good of his firm." Laughter broke out aga
with a note of relief. Mr. MacDougall said, "We could d
with more poison here," and suddenly the dog began
whimper. It broke cover and made for the service-doo
"Max," the head-waiter exclaimed. "Max." There w
silence and then a few uneasy laughs. The dog was unce
tain on its feet. It howled and tried to bite its own breas
The head-waiter overtook it by the door and picked it u
but it cried as though with pain and broke from his arn
"It's had a couple," Mr. MacDougall said uneasily.

"You must excuse me, Dr. Braun," Wormold said, "tl
show is over." He followed the head-waiter through tl
service-door. "Stop."

"What do you want?"

"I want to find out what happened to my plate."

"What do you mean, sir? Your plate?"

"You were very anxious that my plate should not l
given to anyone else."

"I don't understand."

"Did you know that it was poisoned?"

"You mean the food was bad, sir?"

"I mean it was poisoned and you were careful to save Dr. Braun's life—not mine."

"I'm afraid, sir, I don't understand you. I am busy. You must excuse me." The sound of a howling dog came up the long passage from the kitchen, a low dismal howl intercepted by a sharper burst of pain. The head-waiter called, "Max!" and ran like a human being down the passage. He flung open the kitchen-door. "Max!"

The daschshund lifted a melancholy head from where it crouched below the table, then began to drag its body painfully towards the head-waiter. A man in a chef's cap said, "He ate nothing here. The plate was thrown away." The dog collapsed at the waiter's feet and lay there like a length of offal.

The waiter went down on his knees beside the dog. He said, "Max *mein Kind. Mein Kind.*" The black body was like an elongation of his own black suit. The kitchen-staff gathered around.

The black tube made a slight movement and a pink tongue came out like tooth-paste and lay on the kitchen floor. The head-waiter put his hand on the dog and then looked up at Wormold. The tear-filled eyes so accused him of standing there alive while the dog was dead that he nearly found it in his heart to apologise, but instead he turned and went. At the end of the passage he looked back: the black figure knelt beside the black dog and the white chef stood above and the kitchen-hands waited, like mourners round a grave, carrying their troughs and mops and dishes like wreaths. My death, he thought, would have been more unobtrusive than that.

iv

"I have come back," he said to Beatrice, "I am not under the table. I have come back victorious. The dog it was that died."

[4]

i

Captain Segura said, "I'm glad to find you alone. Are you alone?"

"Quite alone."

"I'm sure you don't mind. I have put two men at the door to see that we aren't disturbed."

"Am I under arrest?"

"Of course not."

"Milly and Beatrice are out at a cinema. They'll be surprised if they are not allowed in."

"I will not take up much of your time. There are two things I have come to see you about. One is important. The other is only routine. May I begin with what is important?"

"Please."

"I wish, Mr. Wormold, to ask for the hand of your daughter."

"Does that require two policemen at the door?"

"It's convenient not to be disturbed."

"Have you spoken to Milly?"

"I would not dream of it before speaking to you."

"I suppose even here you *would* need my consent by law."

"It is not a matter of law but of common courtesy. May I smoke?"

"Why not? Is that case really made from human skin?"

Captain Segura laughed. "Ah, Milly, Milly. What a tease she is!" He added ambiguously, "Do you really believe that story, Mr. Wormold?" Perhaps he had an objection to a direct lie; he might be a good Catholic.

"She's much too young to marry, Captain Segura."

"Not in this country."

"I'm sure she has no wish to marry yet."

182

"But you could influence her, Mr. Wormold."

"They call you the Red Vulture, don't they?"

"That, in Cuba, is a kind of compliment."

"Aren't you rather an uncertain life? You seem to have a lot of enemies."

"I have saved enough to take care of my widow. In that way, Mr. Wormold, I am a more reliable support than you are. This establishment—it can't bring you in much money and at any moment it is liable to be closed."

"Closed?"

"I am sure you do not intend to cause trouble, but a lot of trouble has been happening around you. If you had to leave this country, would you not feel happier if your daughter were well established here?"

"What kind of trouble, Captain Segura?"

"There was a car which crashed—never mind why. There was an attack on poor Engineer Cifuentes—a friend of the Minister of the Interior. Professor Sanchez complained that you broke into his house and threatened him. There is even a story that you poisoned a dog."

"That I poisoned a dog?"

"It sounds absurd, of course. But the head-waiter at the Hotel Nacional said you gave his dog poisoned whisky. Why should you give a dog whisky at all? I don't understand. Nor does he. He thinks perhaps because it was a German dog. You don't say anything, Mr. Wormold."

"I am at a loss for words."

"He was in a terrible state, poor man. Otherwise I would have thrown him out of the office for talking nonsense. He said you came into the kitchen to gloat over what you had done. It sounded very unlike you, Mr. Wormold. I have always thought of you as a humane man. Just assure me there is no truth in this story . . ."

"The dog *was* poisoned. The whisky came from my glass. But it was intended for me, not the dog."

"Why should anyone try to poison you?"

"I don't know."

"Two strange stories—they cancel out. Probably there was no poison and the dog just died. I gather it was an old

dog. But you must admit, Mr. Wormold, that a lot c
trouble seems to go on around you. Perhaps you are lik
one of those innocent children I have read about in you
country who set poltergeists to work."

"Perhaps I am. Do you know the names of the polter
geists?"

"Most of them. I think the time has come to exorcis
them. I am drawing up a report for the President."

"Am I on it?"

"You needn't be. I ought to tell you, Mr. Wormol
that I have saved money, enough money to leave Milly i
comfort if anything were ever to happen to me. And c
course enough for us to settle in Miami if there were
revolution."

"There's no need for you to tell me all this. I'm nc
questioning your financial capacity."

"It is customary, Mr. Wormold. Now for my health—
that is good. I can show you the certificates. Nor will the
be any difficulty about children. That has been ampl
proved."

"I see."

"There is nothing in that which need worry you
daughter. The children are provided for. My present er
cumbrance is not an important one. I know that Prot
estants are rather particular about these things."

"I'm not exactly a Protestant."

"And luckily your daughter is a Catholic. It woul
really be a most suitable marriage, Mr. Wormold."

"Milly is only seventeen."

"It is the best and easiest age to bear a child, M
Wormold. Have I your permission to speak to her?"

"Do you need it?"

"It is more correct."

"And if I said no . . . ?"

"I would of course try to persuade you."

"You said once that I was not of the torturabl
class."

Captain Segura laid his hand affectionately on Wor
mold's shoulders. "You have Milly's sense of humour. Bu

seriously, there is always your residence-permit to consider."

"You seem very determined. All right. You may as well speak to her. You have plenty of opportunity on her way from school. But Milly's got sense. I don't think you stand a chance."

"In that case I may ask you later to use a father's influence."

"How Victorian you are, Captain Segura. A father today has no influence. You said there was something important . . ."

Captain Segura said reproachfully, "This was the important subject. The other is a matter of routine only. Would you come with me to the Wonder Bar?"

"Why?"

"A police matter. Nothing for you to worry about. I am asking you a favour, that is all, Mr. Wormold."

They went in Captain Segura's scarlet sports-car with a motor-cycle policeman before and behind. All the bootblacks from the Paseo seemed to be gathered in Virdudes. There were policemen on either side of the swing-doors of the Wonder Bar and the sun lay heavy overhead.

The motor-cycle policemen leapt off their machines and began to shoo the bootblacks away. Policemen ran out from the bar and formed an escort for Captain Segura. Wormold followed him. As always at that time of day, the jalousies above the colonnade were creaking in the small wind from the sea. The barman stood on the wrong side of the bar, the customers' side. He looked sick and afraid. Several broken bottles behind him were still dripping single drops, but they had spilt their main contents a long while ago. Someone on the floor was hidden by the bodies of the policemen, but the boots showed—the thick over-repaired boots of a not-rich old man. "It's just a formal identification," Captain Segura said. Wormold hardly needed to see the face, but they cleared a way before him so that he could look down at Dr. Hasselbacher.

"It's Dr. Hasselbacher," he said. "You know him as well as I do."

"There is a form to be observed in these matters," Segura said. "An independent identification."

"Who did it?"

Segura said, "Who knows? You had better have a glass of whisky. Barman!"

"No. Give me a daiquiri. It was always a daiquri I used to drink with him."

"Someone came in here with a gun. Two shots missed. Of course we shall say it was the rebels from Oriente. It will be useful in influencing foreign opinion. Perhaps it was the rebels."

The face stared up from the floor without expression. You couldn't describe that impassivity in terms of peace or anguish. It was as though nothing at all had ever happened to it: an unborn face.

"When you bury him put his helmet on the coffin."

"Helmet?"

"You'll find an old uniform in his flat. He was a sentimental man." It was odd that Dr. Hasselbacher had survived two world wars and had died at the end of it in so-called peace much the same death as he might have died upon the Somme.

"You know very well it had nothing to do with the rebels," Wormold said.

"It is convenient to say so."

"The poltergeists again."

"You blame yourself too much."

"He warned me not to go to the lunch, Carter heard him, everybody heard him, so they killed him."

"Who are They?"

"You have the list."

"The name Carter wasn't on it."

"Ask the waiter with the dog, then. You can torture *him* surely. I won't complain."

"He is German and he has high political friends. Why should he want to poison you?"

"Because they think I'm dangerous. Me! They little know. Give me another daiquiri. I always had two before I went back to the shop. Will you show me your list, Segura?"

"I might to a father-in-law, because I could trust him."

They can print statistics and count the populations in hundreds of thousands, but to each man a city consists of no more than a few streets, a few houses, a few people. Remove those few and a city exists no longer except as a pain in the memory, like the pain of an amputated leg no longer there. It was time, Wormold thought, to pack up and go and leave the ruins of Havana.

"You know," Captain Segura said, "this only emphasises what I meant. It might have been you. Milly should be safe from accidents like this."

"Yes," Wormold said. "I shall have to see to that."

ii

The policemen were gone from the shop when he returned. Lopez was out, he had no idea where. He could hear Rudy fidgeting with his tubes and an occasional snatch of atmospherics beat around the apartment. He sat down on the bed. Three deaths: an unknown man called Raul, a black dachshund called Max and an old doctor called Hasselbacher; he was the cause—and Carter. Carter had not planned the death of Raul nor the dog, but Dr. Hasselbacher had been given no chance. It had been a reprisal: one death for one life, a reversal of the Mosaic Code. He could hear Milly and Beatrice talking in the next room. Although the door was ajar he only half took in what they were saying. He stood on the frontier of violence, a strange land he had never visited before; he had his passport in his hand. "Profession: Spy." "Characteristic Features: Friendlessness." "Purpose of Visit: Murder." No visa was required. His papers were in order.

And on this side of the border he heard the voices talking in the language he knew.

Beatrice said, "No, I wouldn't advise deep carnation. Not at your age."

Milly said, "They ought to give lessons in make-up during the last term. I can just hear Sister Agnes saying, 'A drop of *Nuit d'Amour* behind the ears.'"

"Try this light carnation. No, don't smear the edge of your mouth. Let me show you."

Wormold thought, I have no arsenic or cyanide. Besides I will have no opportunity to drink with him. I should have forced that whisky down his throat. Easier said than done off the Elizabethan stage, and even there he would have needed in addition a poisoned rapier.

"There. You see what I mean."

"What about rouge?"

"You don't need rouge."

"What smell do you use, Beatrice?"

"*Sous Le Vent.*"

They have shot Hasselbacher, but I have no gun, Wormold thought. Surely a gun should have been part of the office-equipment, like the safe and the celluloid sheets and the microscope and the electric kettle. He had never in his life so much as handled a gun, but that was no insuperable objection. He had only to be as close to Carter as the door through which the voices came.

"We'll go shopping together. I think you'd like *Indiscret*. That's Lelong."

"It doesn't sound very passionate," Milly said.

"You are young. You don't have to put passion on behind the ears."

"You must give a man encouragement," Milly said.

"Just look at him."

"Like this?" Wormold heard Beatrice laugh. He looked at the door with astonishment. He had gone in thought so far across the border that he had forgotten he was still here on this side with them.

"You needn't give them all that encouragement," Beatrice said.

"Did I languish?"

"I'd call it smoulder."

"Do you miss being married?" Milly asked.

"If you mean do I miss Peter, I don't."

"If he died would you marry again?"

"I don't think I'd wait for that. He's only forty."

"Oh yes. I suppose *you* could marry again, if you call it marriage."

"I do."

"But it's terrible, isn't it. *I* have to marry for keeps."

"Most of us think we are going to do that—when we do it."

"I'd be much better off as a mistress."

"I don't believe your father would like that very much."

"I don't see why not. If he married again it wouldn't be any different. She'd really be his mistress, wouldn't she? He wanted to stay with Mother always. I know. He told me so. It was a real marriage. Even a good pagan can't get round that."

"I thought the same about Peter. Milly, Milly, don't let them make you hard."

"They?"

"The nuns."

"Oh. They don't talk to me that way. Not that way at all."

There was always, of course, the possibility of a knife. But for a knife you had to be closer to Carter than he could ever hope to get.

Milly said, "Do you love my father?"

He thought: One day I can come back and settle these questions. But now there are more important problems; I have to discover how to kill a man. Surely they produced handbooks to tell you that? There must be treatises on unarmed combat. He looked at his hands, but he didn't trust them.

Beatrice said, "Why do you ask that?"

"A way you looked at him."

"When?"

"When he came back from that lunch. Perhaps you were just pleased because he'd made a speech?"

"Yes."

"It wouldn't do," Milly said. "I mean, you loving him."

Wormold said to himself, At least if I could kill him, I would kill for a clean reason. I would kill to show that you can't kill without being killed in your turn. I wouldn't kill for my country. I wouldn't kill for capitalism or

Communism or social democracy or the welfare state—whose welfare? I would kill Carter because he killed Hasselbacher. A family-feud had been a better reason for murder than patriotism or the preference for one economic system over another. If I love or if I hate, let me love or hate as an individual. I will not be 59200/5 in anyone's global war.

"If I loved him, why shouldn't I?"

"He's married."

"Milly, dear Milly. Beware of formulas. If there's a God, he's not a God of formulas."

"Do you love him?"

"I never said so."

A gun is the only way; where can I get a gun?

Somebody came through the door; he didn't even look up. Rudy's tubes gave a high shriek in the next room. Milly's voice said, "We didn't hear you come in."

He said, "I want you to do something for me, Milly."

"Were you listening?"

He heard Beatrice say, "What's wrong? What's happened?"

"There's been an accident, a kind of accident."

"Who?"

"Dr. Hasselbacher."

"Serious?"

"Yes."

"You are breaking the news, aren't you?" Milly said.

"Yes."

"Poor Dr. Hasselbacher."

"Yes."

"I'll get the chaplain to say a Mass for every year we knew him." There hadn't, he realised, been any need to break a death gently, so far as Milly was concerned. All deaths to her were happy deaths. Vengeance was unnecessary when you believed in a heaven. But he had no such belief. Mercy and forgiveness were scarcely virtues in a Christian; they came too easily.

He said, "Captain Segura was here. He wants you to marry him."

"That old man. I'll never ride in his car again."

"I'd like you to once more, tomorrow. Tell him I want to see him."

"Why?"

"A game of draughts. At ten o'clock. You and Beatrice must be out of the way."

"Will he pester me?"

"No. Just tell him to come and talk to me. Tell him to bring his list. He'll understand."

"And afterwards?"

"We are going home. To England."

When he was alone with Beatrice, he said, "That's that. The end of the office."

"What do you mean?"

"Perhaps we'll go down gloriously with one good report—the list of secret agents operating here."

"Including us?"

"Oh no. We've never operated."

"I don't understand."

"I've got no agents, Beatrice. Not one. Hasselbacher was killed for no reason. There are no constructions in the Oriente mountains."

It was typical of her that she showed no incredulity. This was a piece of information like any other information to be filed for reference. Any assessment of its value would be made, he thought, by the head-office.

He said, "Of course it's your duty to report this immediately to London, but I'd be grateful if you'd wait till after tomorrow. We may be able to add something genuine then."

"If you are alive, you mean."

"Of course I'll be alive."

"You are planning something."

"Segura has the list of agents."

"That's not what you are planning. But if you are dead," she said with what sounded like anger, *"de mortuis* I suppose."

"If something did happen to me I wouldn't want you to learn for the first time from these bogus files what a fraud I'd been."

"But Raul . . . there must have been a Raul."

"Poor man. He must have wondered what was happening to him. Taking a joy-ride in his usual way. Perhaps he was drunk in his usual way too. I hope so."

"But he existed."

"One has to get a name from somewhere. I must have picked his up without remembering it."

"Those diagrams?"

"I drew them myself from the Atomic Pile Cleaner. The joke's over now. Would you like to write out a confession for me to sign? I'm glad they didn't do anything serious to Teresa."

She began to laugh. She put her head in her hands and laughed. She said, "Oh, how I love you."

"It must seem pretty silly to you."

"London seems pretty silly. And Henry Hawthorne. Do you think I would ever have left Peter if once—just once—he'd made a fool of UNESCO? But UNESCO was sacred. Cultural conferences were sacred. He never laughed . . . Lend me your handkerchief."

"You're crying."

"I'm laughing. Those drawings . . ."

"One was a nozzle-spray and another was a double-action coupling. I never thought they would pass the experts."

"They weren't seen by experts. You forget—this is a Secret Service. We have to protect our sources. We can't allow documents like that to reach anyone who really knows. Darling . . ."

"You said darling."

"It's a way of speaking. Do you remember the Tropicana and that man singing? I didn't know you were my boss and I was your secretary, you were just a nice man with a lovely daughter and I knew you wanted to do something crazy with a champagne bottle and I was so deadly bored with sense . . ."

"But I'm not the crazy type."

> They say the earth is round—
> My madness offends.

"I wouldn't be a seller of vacuum cleaners if I were the crazy type."

> I say that night is day
> And I've no axe to grind.

"Haven't you any more loyalty than I have?"

"You are loyal."

"Who to?"

"To Milly. I don't care a damn about men who are loyal to the people who pay them, to organisations . . . I don't think even my country means all that much. There are many countries in our blood, aren't there, but only one person. Would the world be in the mess it is if we were loyal to love and not to countries?"

He said, "I suppose they could take away my passport."

"Let them try."

"All the same," he said, "it's the end of a job for both of us."

[5]

i

"Come in, Captain Segura."

Captain Segura gleamed. His leather gleamed, his buttons gleamed, and there was fresh pomade upon his hair. He was like a well-cared-for weapon. He said, "I was so pleased when Milly brought the message."

"We have a lot to talk over. Shall we have a game first? Tonight I am going to beat you."

"I doubt it, Mr. Wormold. I do not yet have to show you filial respect."

Wormold unfolded the draughts board. Then he arranged on the board twenty-four miniature bottles of whisky: twelve Bourbon confronted twelve Scotch.

"What is this, Mr. Wormold?"

"An idea of Dr. Hasselbacher's. I thought we might have one game to his memory. When you take a piece you drink it."

"A shrewd idea, Mr. Wormold. As I am the better player I drink more."

"And then I catch up with you—in the drinks also."

"I think I would prefer to play with ordinary pieces."

"Are you afraid of being beaten, Segura? Perhaps you have a weak head."

"My head is as strong as another man's, but sometimes with drink I lose my temper. I do not wish to lose my temper with my future father."

"Milly won't marry you, Segura."

"That is what we have to discuss."

"You play with the Bourbon. Bourbon is stronger than Scotch. I shall be handicapped."

"That is not necessary. I will play with the Scotch."

Segura turned the board and sat down.

"Why not take off your belt, Segura? You'll be more comfortable."

Segura laid his belt and holster on the ground beside him. "I will fight you unarmed," he said jovially.

"Do you keep your gun loaded?"

"Of course. The kind of enemies I possess do not give me a chance to load."

"Have you found the murderer of Hasselbacher?"

"No. He does not belong to the criminal class."

"Carter?"

"After what you said, naturally I checked. He was with Dr. Braun at the time. And we cannot doubt the word of the President of the European Traders' Association, can we?"

"So Dr. Braun is on your list?"

"Naturally. And now to play."

There is an imaginary line in draughts, as every player knows, that crosses the board diagonally from corner to corner. It is the line of defence. Whoever gains control of that line takes the initiative; when the line is crossed the attack has begun. With an insolent ease Segura estab-

lished himself with a Defiance opening, then moved a
bottle across through the centre of the board. He didn't
hesitate between moves; he hardly looked at the board. It
was Wormold who paused and thought.

"Where is Milly?" Segura asked.

"Out."

"And your charming secretary?"

"With Milly."

"You are already in difficulties," Captain Segura said.
He struck at the base of Wormold's defence and captured
a bottle of Old Taylor. "The first drink," he said and
drained it. Wormold recklessly began a pincer-movement
in reply and almost at once lost a bottle—of Old Forester
this time. A few beads of sweat came out on Segura's
forehead and he cleared his throat after drinking. He
said, "You play recklessly, Mr. Wormold." He indicated
the board. "You should have taken that piece."

"You can huff me," Wormold said.

For the first time Segura hesitated. He said, "No. I
prefer you to take my piece." It was an unfamiliar whisky
called Cairngorm and it found a raw spot on Wormold's
tongue.

They played for a while with exaggerated care, neither
taking a piece.

"Is Carter still at the Seville-Biltmore?" Wormold
asked.

"Yes."

"Do you keep him under observation?"

"No. What is the use?"

Wormold was clinging to the edge of the board with
what was left of his foiled pincer-movement, but he had
lost his base. He made a false move which enabled Segura
to thrust a protected piece into square 22 and there was
no way left of saving his piece on 25 and preventing
Segura from reaching the back row and gaining a king.

"Careless," Segura said.

"I can make it an exchange."

"But I have the king."

Segura drank a Four Roses and Wormold at the other

end of the board took a dimpled Haig. Segura said, "It is a hot evening." He crowned his king with a scrap of paper. Wormold said, "If I capture him I have to drink two bottles. I have spares in the cupboard."

"You have thought everything out," Segura said. Was it with sourness?

He played now with great caution. It became difficult to tempt him to a capture and Wormold began to realise the fundamental weakness of his plan, that it is possible for a good player to defeat an opponent without capturing his pieces. He took one more of Segura's and was trapped. He was left without a move.

Segura wiped the sweat from his forehead. "You see," he said, "you cannot win."

"You must give me my revenge."

"This Bourbon is strong. 85 proof."

"We will switch the whiskies."

This time Wormold was black, with the Scotch. He had replaced the three Scotch he had drunk and the three Bourbon. He started with the Old Fourteenth opening, which is apt to lead to a long-drawn-out game, for he knew now that his only hope was to make Segura lose his caution and play for pieces. Again he tried to be huffed, but Segura would not accept the move. It was as though Segura had recognised that his real opponent was not Wormold but his own head. He even threw away a piece with no tactical advantage and forced Wormold to take it—a Hiram Walker. Wormold realised that his own head was in danger; the mixture of Scotch and Bourbon was a deadly one. He said, "Give me a cigarette." Segura leant forward to light it and Wormold was aware of the effort he had to make to keep the lighter steady. It wouldn't snap and he cursed with unnecessary violence. Two more drinks and I have him, Wormold thought.

But it was as difficult to lose a piece to an unwilling antagonist as to capture one. Against his own will the battle was swaying to his side. He drank one Harper's and made a king. He said with false joviality, "The game's mine, Segura. Do you want to pack up?"

Segura scowled at the board. It was obvious that he was torn in two, between the desire to win and the desire to keep his head, but his head was clouded by anger as well as whisky. He said, "This is a pig's way of playing checkers." Now that his opponent had a king, he could no longer play for a bloodless victory, for the king had freedom of movement. This time when he sacrificed a Kentucky Tavern it was a genuine sacrifice and he swore at the pieces. "The damned shapes," he said, "They are all different. Cut-glass, whoever heard of a checker-piece of cut-glass?" Wormold felt his own brain fogged with the Bourbon, but the moment for victory—and defeat—had come.

Segura said, "You moved my piece."

"No, that's Red Label. Mine."

"How in God's name can I tell the difference between Scotch and Bourbon? They are all bottles, aren't they?"

"You are angry because you are losing."

"I never lose."

Then Wormold made his careful slip and exposed his king. For a moment he thought that Segura had not noticed and then he thought that deliberately to avoid drinking Segura was going to let his chance go by. But the temptation to take the king was great and what lay beyond the move was a shattering victory. His own piece would be made a king and a massacre would follow. Yet he hesitated. The heat of the whisky and the close night melted his face like a wax doll's; he had difficulty in focusing. He said, "Why did you do that?"

"What?"

"You lose your king an' the game."

"Damn. I didn't notice. I must be drunk."

"You drunk?"

"A little."

"I'm drunk too. You know I'm drunk. You are trying to make me drunk. Why?"

"Don't be a fool, Segura. Why should I want to make you drunk? Let's stop the game, call it a draw."

"God damn a draw. I know why you want to make me

drunk. You want to show me that list—I mean you want me to show you."

"What list?"

"I have you all in the net. Where is Milly?"

"I told you, out."

"Tonight I go to the Chief of Police. We draw the net tight."

"With Carter in it?"

"Who is Carter?" He wagged his finger at Wormold. "You are in it—but I know you are no agent. You are a fraud."

"Why not sleep a bit, Segura? A drawn game."

"No drawn game. Look. I take your king." He opened the little bottle of Red Label and drank it down.

"Two bottles for a king," Wormold said and handed him a Dunosdale Cream.

Segura sat heavily in his chair, his chin rocking. He said, "Admit you are beaten. I do not play for pieces."

"I admit nothing. I have the better head and look, I huff you. You could have gone on." A Canadian rye had got mixed with the Bourbons, a Lord Calvert, and Wormold drank it down. He thought, it must be the last. If he doesn't pass out now, I'm finished. I won't be sober enough to pull a trigger. Did he say it was loaded?

"Matters nothing," Segura said in a whisper. "You are finished anyway." He moved his hand slowly over the board as though he were carrying an egg in a spoon. "See?" He captured one piece, two pieces, three . . .

"Drink this, Segura." A George IV, a Queen Anne, the game was ending in a flourish of royalty, a Highland Queen.

"You can go on, Segura. Or shall I huff you again? Drink it down." Vat 69. "Another. Drink it, Segura." Grant's Standfast. Old Argyll. "Drink them, Segura. I surrender now." But it was Segura who had surrendered. Wormold undid the captain's collar to give him air and eased his head on the back of the seat, but his own legs were uncertain as he walked towards the door. He had Segura's gun in his pocket.

ii

At the Seville-Biltmore he went to the house-phone and called up Carter. He had to admit that Carter's nerves were steady—far steadier than his own. Carter's mission in Cuba had not been properly fulfilled and yet he stayed on, as a marksman or perhaps as a decoy duck. Wormold said, "Good evening, Carter."

"Why, good evening, Wormold." The voice had just the right chill of injured pride.

"I want to apologise to you, Carter. That silly business of the whisky. I was tight I suppose. I'm a bit tight now. Not used to apologising."

"It's quite all right, Wormold. Go to bed."

"Sneered at your stammer. Chap shouldn't do that." He found himself talking like Hawthorne. Falsity was an occupational disease.

"I didn't know what the H-hell you meant."

"I shoon—soon—found out what was wrong. Nothing to do with you. That damned head-waiter poisoned his own dog. It was very old, of course, but to give it poisoned scraps—that's not the way to put a dog to sleep."

"Is that what h-happened? Thank you for letting me know, but it's late. I'm just going to bed, Wormold."

"Man's best friend."

"What's that? I can't h-hear you."

"Caesar, the King's friend, and there was the rough-haired one who went down at Jutland. Last seen on the bridge beside his master."

"You are drunk, Wormold." It was so much easier, Wormold found, to imitate drunkenness after—how many Scotch and Bourbon? You can trust a drunk man—*in vino veritas*. You can also more easily dispose of a drunk man. Carter would be a fool not to take the chance. Wormold said, "I feel in the mood for going round the spots."

"What spots?"

"The spots you wanted to see in Havana."

"It's getting late."

"It's the right time." Carter's hesitation came at him down the wire. He said, "Bring a gun." He felt a strange reluctance to kill an unarmed killer—if Carter should ever chance to be unarmed.

"A gun? Why?"

"In some of these places they try to roll you."

"Can't *you* bring one?"

"I don't happen to own one."

"Nor do I," and he believed he caught in the receiver the metallic sound of a chamber being checked. Diamond cut diamond, he thought, and smiled. But a smile is dangerous to the act of hate as much as to the act of love. He had to remind himself of how Hasselbacher had looked, staring up from the floor under the bar. They had not given the old man one chance, and he was giving Carter plenty. He began to regret the drinks he had taken.

"I'll meet you in the bar," Carter said.

"Don't be long."

"I have to get dressed."

Wormold was glad now of the darkness of the bar. Carter, he supposed, was telephoning to his friends and perhaps making a rendezvous, but in the bar at any rate they couldn't pick him out before he saw them. There was one entrance from the street and one from the hotel, and at the back a kind of balcony which would give support if he needed it to his gun. Anyone who entered was blinded for a while by the darkness, as he himself was. When he entered he couldn't for a moment see whether the bar held one or two customers, for the pair were tightly locked on a sofa by the street-door.

He asked for a Scotch, but he left it untasted, sitting on the balcony, watching both doors. Presently a man entered; he couldn't see the face; it was the hand patting the pipe-pocket which identified Carter.

"Carter."

Carter came to him.

"Let's be off," Wormold said.

"Take your drink first and I'll h-have one to keep you company."

"I've had too much, Carter. I need some air. We'll get a drink in some house."

Carter sat down. "Tell me where you plan to take me."

"Any one of a dozen whore-houses. They are all the same, Carter. About a dozen girls to choose from. They'll do an exhibition for you. Come on, we'll go. They get crowded after midnight."

Carter said anxiously, "I'd like a drink first. I can't go to a show like that stone sober."

"You aren't expecting anyone, are you, Carter?"

"No, why?"

"I thought—the way you watched the door . . ."

"I don't know a soul in this town. I told you."

"Except Dr. Braun."

"Oh yes, of course, Dr. Braun. But he's not the kind of companion to take to a h-house, is he?"

"After you, Carter."

Reluctantly Carter moved. It was obvious that he was searching for an excuse to stay. He said, "I just want to leave a message with the porter. I'm expecting a telephone call."

"From Dr. Braun?"

"Yes." He hesitated. "It seems rude going out like this before h-he rings. Can't you wait five minutes, Wormold?"

"Say you'll be back by one—unless you decide to make a night of it."

"It would be better to wait."

"Then I'll go without you. Damn you, Carter, I thought you wanted to see the town." He walked rapidly away. His car was parked across the street. He never looked back, but he heard steps following him. Carter no more wanted to lose him than he wanted to lose Carter.

"What a temper you've got, Wormold."

"I'm sorry. Drink takes me that way."

"I h-hope you are sober enough to drive straight."

"It would be better, Carter, if you drove."

He thought, That will keep his hands from his pockets.

"First right, first left, Carter."

They came out into the Atlantic drive: a lean white ship was leaving harbour, some tourist-cruiser bound for Kingston or for Port au Prince. They could see the couples leaning over the rail, romantic in the moonlight, and a band was playing a fading favourite—"*I could have danced all night.*"

"It makes me homesick," Carter said.

"For Nottwich?"

"Yes."

"There's no sea at Nottwich."

"The pleasure-boats on the river looked as big as that when I was young."

A murderer had no right to be homesick; a murderer should be a machine, and I too have to become a machine, Wormold thought, feeling in his pocket the handkerchief he would have to use to clean the fingerprints when the time came. But how to choose the time? What side-street or what doorway? and if the other shot first . . . ?

"Are your friends Russian, Carter? German? American?"

"What friends?" He added simply, "I have no friends."

"No friends?"

"No."

"To the left again, Carter, then right."

They moved at a walking pace now in a narrow street, lined with clubs; orchestras spoke from below ground like the ghost of Hamlet's father or that music under the paving stones in Alexandria when the god Hercules left Antony. Two men in Cuban night-club uniform bawled competitively to them across the road. Wormold said, "Let's stop. I need a drink badly before we go on."

"Are these whore-houses?"

"No. We'll go to a house later." He thought, If only Carter when he left the wheel had grabbed his gun, it would have been so easy to fire. Carter said, "Do you know this spot?"

"No. But I know the tune." It was strange that they were playing that—"my madness offends."

There were coloured photographs of naked girls outside and in night-club Esperanto one neon-lighted word, Strippteese. Steps painted in stripes like cheap pyjamas led them down towards a cellar foggy with Havanas. It seemed as suitable a place as any other for an execution. But he wanted a drink first. "You lead the way, Carter." Carter was hesitating. He opened his mouth and struggled with an aspirate; Wormold had never before heard him struggle for quite so long. "I h-h-h-hope . . ."

"What do you hope?"

"Nothing."

They sat and watched the stripping and both drank brandy and soda. A girl went from table to table ridding herself of clothes. She began with her gloves. A spectator took them wih resignation like the contents of an In tray. Then she presented her back to Carter and told him to unhook her black lace corsets. Carter fumbled in vain at the catches, blushing all the time while the girl laughed and wriggled against his fingers. He said, "I'm sorry, I can't find . . ." Round the floor the gloomy men sat at their little tables watching Carter. No one smiled.

"You haven't had much practice, Carter, in Nottwich. Let me."

"Leave me alone, can't you?"

At last he got the corset undone and the girl rumpled his thin streaky hair and passed on. He smoothed it down again with a pocket-comb. "I don't like this place," he said.

"You are shy with women, Carter." But how could one shoot a man at whom it was so easy to laugh?

"I don't like horseplay," Carter said.

They climbed the stairs. Carter's pocket was heavy on his hip. Of course it might be his pipe he carried. He sat at the wheel again and grumbled. "You can see that sort of show anywhere. Just tarts undressing."

"You didn't help her much."

"I was looking for a zip."

"I needed a drink badly."

"Rotten brandy too. I wouldn't wonder if it was doped."

"Your whisky was more than doped, Carter." He was trying to heat his anger up and not to remember his ineffective victim struggling with the corset and blushing at his failure.

"What's that you said?"

"Stop here."

"Why?"

"You wanted to be taken to a house. Here is a house."

"But there's no one about."

"They are all closed and shuttered like this. Get out and ring the bell."

"What did you mean about the whisky?"

"Never mind that now. Get out and ring."

It was as suitable a place as a cellar (blank walls too had been frequently used for this purpose): a grey façade and a street where no one came except for one unlovely purpose. Carter slowly shifted his legs from under the wheel and Wormold watched his hands closely, the ineffective hands. It's a fair duel, he told himself, he's more accustomed to killing than I am, the chances are equal enough; I am not even quite sure my gun is loaded. He has more chance than Hasselbacher ever had.

With his hand on the door Carter paused again. He said, "Perhaps it would be more sensible—some other night. You know, I h-h-h-h . . ."

"You are frightened, Carter."

"I've never been to a h-h-h-house before. To tell you the truth, Wormold, I don't h-have much need of women."

"It sounds a lonely sort of life."

"I can do without them," he said defiantly. "There are more important things for a man than running after . . ."

"Why did you want to come to a house then?"

Again he startled Wormold with the plain truth. "I try to want them, but when it comes to the point . . ." He hovered on the edge of confession and then plunged. "It doesn't work, Wormold. I can't do what they want."

"Get out of the car."

I have to do it, Wormold thought, before he confesses any more to me. With every second the man was becoming human, a creature like oneself whom one might pity or console, not kill. Who knew what excuses were buried below any violent act? He drew Segura's gun.

"What?"

"Get out."

Carter stood against the whore-house door with a look of sullen complaint rather than fear. His fear was of women, not of violence. He said, "You are making a mistake. It was Braun who gave me the whisky. I'm not important."

"I don't care about the whisky. But you killed Hasselbacher, didn't you?"

Again he surprised Wormold with the truth. There was a kind of honesty in the man. "I was under orders, Wormold. I h-h-h-h——" He had manœuvred himself so that his elbow reached the bell, and now he leant back and in the depths of the house the bell rang and rang its summons to work.

"There's no enmity, Wormold. You got too dangerous, that was all. We are only private soldiers, you and I."

"Me dangerous? What fools you people must be. I have no agents, Carter."

"Oh yes, you h-have. Those constructions in the mountains. We have copies of your drawings."

"The parts of a vacuum cleaner." He wondered who had supplied them: Lopez? or Hawthorne's own courier, or a man in the Consulate?

Carter's hand went to his pocket and Wormold fired. Carter gave a sharp yelp. He said, "You nearly shot me," and pulled out a hand clasped round a shattered pipe. He said, "My Dunhill. You've smashed my Dunhill."

"Beginner's luck," Wormold said. He had braced himself for a death, but it was impossible to shoot again. The door behind Carter began to open. There was an impression of plastic music. "They'll look after you in there. You may need a woman now, Carter."

"You—you clown."

How right Carter was. He put the gun down beside him and slipped into the driving seat. Suddenly he felt happy. He might have killed a man. He had proved conclusively to himself that he wasn't one of the judges; he had no vocation for violence. Then Carter fired.

[6]

i

He said to Beatrice, "I was just leaning forward to switch on the engine. That saved me, I imagine. Of course it was his right to fire back. It was a real duel, but the third shot was mine."

"What happened afterwards?"

"I had time to drive away before I was sick."

"Sick?"

"I suppose if I hadn't missed the war it would have seemed much less serious a thing killing a man. Poor Carter."

"Why should you feel sorry for him?"

"He was a man. I'd learnt a lot about him. He couldn't undo a girl's corset. He was scared of women. He liked his pipe and when he was a boy the pleasure-steamers on the river at home seemed to him like liners. Perhaps he was a romantic. A romantic is usually afraid, isn't he, in case reality doesn't come up to expectations. They all expect too much."

"And then?"

"I wiped my prints off the gun and brought it back. Of course Segura will find that two shots have been fired. But I don't suppose he'll want to claim the bullets. It would be a little difficult to explain. He was still asleep when I came in. I'm afraid to think what a head he'll have now. My own is bad enough. But I tried to follow your instructions with the photograph."

"What photograph?"

"He had a list of foreign agents he was taking to the Chief of Police. I photographed it and put it back in his pocket. I'm glad to feel there's one real report that I've sent before I resign."

"You should have waited for me."

"How could I? He was going to wake at any moment. But this micro business is tricky."

"Why on earth did you make a microphotograph?"

"Because we can't trust any courier to Kingston. Carter's people—whoever they are—have copies of the Oriente drawings. That means a double agent somewhere. Perhaps it's your man who smuggles in the drugs. So I made a microphotograph as you showed me and I stuck it on the back of a stamp and I posted off an assorted batch of five hundred British colonials, the way we arranged for an emergency."

"We'll have to cable them which stamp you've stuck it to."

"Which stamp?"

"You don't expect them to look through five hundred stamps, do you, looking for one black dot."

"I hadn't thought of that. How very awkward."

"You must know which stamp . . ."

"I didn't think of looking at the front. I think it was a George V, and it was red—or green."

"That's helpful. Do you remember any of the names on the list?"

"No. There wasn't time to read it properly. I know I'm a fool at this game, Beatrice."

"No. They are the fools."

"I wonder whom we'll hear from next. Dr. Braun . . . Segura . . ."

But it was neither of them.

ii

The supercilious clerk from the Consulate appeared in the shop at five o'clock the next afternoon. He stood stiffly among the vacuum cleaners like a disapproving tourist in a museum of phallic objects. He told Wormold that the

Ambassador wanted to see him. "Will tomorrow morning do?" He was working on his last report, Carter's death and his resignation.

"No, it won't. He telephoned from his home. You are to go there straight away."

"I'm not an employee," Wormold said.

"Aren't you?"

Wormold drove back to Vedado, to the little white houses and the bougainvilleas of the rich. It seemed a long while since his visit to Professor Sanchez. He passed the house. What quarrels were still in progress behind those doll's-house walls?

He had a sense that everyone in the Ambassador's home was on the look-out for him and that the hall and the stairs had been carefully cleared of spectators. On the first floor a woman turned her back and shut herself in a room; he thought it was the Ambassadress. Two children peered quickly through the banisters on the second floor and ran off with a click of little heels on the tiled floor. The butler showed him into the drawing-room, which was empty, and closed the door on him stealthily. Through the tall windows he could see a long green lawn and tall sub-tropical trees. Even there somebody was moving rapidly away.

The room was like many Embassy drawing-rooms, a mixture of big inherited pieces and small personal objects acquired in previous stations. Wormold thought he could detect a past in Teheran (an odd-shaped pipe, a tile), Athens (an icon or two), but he was momentarily puzzled by an African mask—perhaps Monrovia?

The Ambassador came in, a tall cold man in a Guards tie, with something about him of what Hawthorne would have liked to be. He said, "Sit down, Wormold. Have a cigarette?"

"No thank you, sir."

"You'll find that chair more comfortable. Now it's no use beating about the bush, Wormold. You are in trouble."

"Yes."

"Of course I know nothing—nothing at all—of what you are doing here."

"I sell vacuum cleaners, sir."

The Ambassador looked at him with undisguised distaste. "Vacuum cleaners? I wasn't referring to them." He looked away from Wormold at the Persian pipe, the Greek icon, the Liberian mask. They were like the autobiography in which a man has written for reassurance only of his better days. He said, "Yesterday morning Captain Segura came to see me. Mind you, I don't know how the police got this information, it's none of my business, but he told you had been sending a lot of reports home of a misleading character. I don't know whom you sent them to: that's none of my business either. He said in fact that you had been drawing money and pretending to have sources of information which simply don't exist. I thought it my duty to inform the Foreign Office at once. I gather you will be receiving orders to go home and report —who to I have no idea, that sort of thing has nothing to do with me." Wormold saw two small heads looking out from behind one of the tall trees. He looked at them and they looked at him, he thought, sympathetically. He said, "Yes, sir?"

"I got the impression that Captain Segura considered you were causing a lot of trouble here. I think if you refused to go home you might find yourself in serious trouble with the authorities, and under the circumstances of course I could do nothing to help you. Nothing at all. Captain Segura even suspects you of having forged some kind of document which he says you claim to have found in his possession. The whole subject is distasteful to me, Wormold. I can't tell you how distasteful it is. The correct sources for information abroad are the embassies. We have our attachés for that purpose. This so-called secret information is a trouble to every ambassador."

"Yes, sir."

"I don't know whether you've heard—it's been kept out of the papers—but an Englishman was shot the night before last. Captain Segura hinted that he was not unconnected with you."

"I met him once at lunch, sir."

"You had better go home, Wormold, on the first plane you can manage—the sooner the better for me—and discuss it with your people—whoever they are."

"Yes, sir."

iii

The K.L.M. plane was due to take off at three-thirty in the morning for Amsterdam by way of Montreal. Wormold had no desire to travel to Kingston, where Hawthorne might have instructions to meet him. The office had been closed with a final cable and Rudy and his suitcase were routed to Jamaica. The code-books were burnt with the help of the celluloid sheets. Beatrice was to go with Rudy. Lopez was left in charge of the vacuum cleaners. All the personal possessions he valued Wormold got into one crate, which he arranged to send by sea. The horse was sold—to Captain Segura.

Beatrice helped him pack. The last object in the crate was the statue of St. Seraphina.

"Milly must be very unhappy," Beatrice said.

"She's wonderfully resigned. She says like Sir Humphrey Gilbert that God is just as close to her in England as in Cuba."

"It wasn't quite what Gilbert said."

There was a pile of unsecret rubbish left to be burnt.

Beatrice said, "What a lot of photographs you had tucked away—of *her*."

"I used to feel it was like killing someone to tear up a photograph. Of course I know now that it's quite different."

"What's this red box?"

"She gave me some cuff-links once. They were stolen, but I kept the box. I don't know why. In a way I'm glad to see all this stuff go."

"The end of a life."

"Of two lives."

"What's this?"

"An old programme."

"Not so old. The Tropicana. May I keep it?"

"You are too young to keep things," Wormold said. "They accumulate too much. Soon you find you have nowhere left to live among the junk-boxes."

"I'll risk it. That was a wonderful evening."

Milly and Wormold saw her off at the airport. Rudy disappeared unobtrusively following the man with the enormous suitcase. It was a hot afternoon and people stood around drinking daiquireis. Ever since Captain Segura's proposal of marriage Milly's duenna had disappeared, but after her disappearance the child, whom he had hoped to see again, who had set fire to Thomas Earl Parkman, Junior, had not returned. It was as though Milly had outgrown both characters simultaneously. She said with grown-up tact, "I want to find some magazines for Beatrice," and busied herself at a bookstall with her back turned.

"I'm sorry," Wormold said. "I'll tell them when I get back that you know nothing. I wonder where you'll be sent next."

"The Persian Gulf perhaps. Basra."

"Why the Persian Gulf?"

"It's their idea of purgatory. Regeneration through sweat and tears. Do Phastkleaners have an agency at Basra?"

"I'm afraid Phastkleaners won't keep me on."

"What will you do?"

"I've got enough, thanks to poor Raul, for Milly's year in Switzerland. After that I don't know."

"You could open one of those practical joke shops— you know, the bloodstained thumb and the spilt ink and the fly on the lump of sugar. How ghastly goings-away are. Please don't wait any longer."

"Shall I see you again?"

"I'll try not to go to Basra. I'll try to stay in the typists' pool with Angelica and Ethel and Miss Jenkinson. When I'm lucky I shall be off at six and we could meet at the Corner House for a cheap snack and go to the movies. It's one of those ghastly lives, isn't it, like UNESCO and modern writers in conference? It's been fun here with you."

"Yes."

"Now go away."

He went to the magazine stall and found Milly. "We're off," he said.

"But, Beatrice—she hasn't got her magazines."

"She doesn't want them."

"I didn't say good-bye."

"Too late. She's passed the emigration now. You'll see her in London. Perhaps."

iv

It was as if they spent all their remaining time in airports. Now it was the K.L.M. flight and it was three in the morning and the sky was pink with the reflection of neon-lighted stands and landing-flares, and it was Captain Segura who was doing the "seeing off." He tried to make the official occasion seem as private as possible, but it was still a little like a deportation. Segura said reproachfully, "You drove me to this."

"Your methods are gentler than Carter's or Dr. Braun's. What are you doing about Dr. Braun?"

"He finds it necessary to return to Switzerland on a matter to do with his precision-instruments."

"With a passage booked on to Moscow?"

"Not necessarily. Perhaps Bonn. Or Washington. Or even Bucharest. I don't know. Whoever they are they are pleased, I believe, with your drawings."

"Drawings?"

"Of the constructions in Oriente. He will also take the credit for getting rid of a dangerous agent."

"Me?"

"Yes. Cuba will be a little quieter without you both, but I shall miss Milly."

"Milly would never have married you, Segura. She doesn't really like cigarette-cases made of human skin."

"Did you ever hear whose skin?"

"No."

"A police-officer who tortured my father to death. You see, he was a poor man. He belonged to the torturable class."

Milly joined them, carrying *Time, Life, Paris-Match* and *Quick*. It was nearly 3:15 and there was a band of grey in the sky over the flare-path where the false dawn had begun. The pilots moved out to the plane and the air-hostesses followed. He knew the three of them by sight; they had sat with Beatrice at the Tropicana weeks ago. A loudspeaker announced in English and Spanish the departure of flight 396 to Montreal and Amsterdam.

"I have a present for each of you," Segura said. He gave them two little packets. They opened them while the plane wheeled over Havana; the chain of lights along the marine parade swung out of sight and the sea fell like a curtain on all that past. In Wormold's packet was a miniature bottle of Grant's Standfast, and a bullet which had been fired from a police-gun. In Milly's was a small silver horseshoe inscribed with her initials.

"Why the bullet?" Milly asked.

"Oh, a joke in rather doubtful taste. All the same, he wasn't a bad chap," Wormold said.

"But not right for a husband," the grown-up Milly replied.

Epilogue in London

i

They had looked at him curiously when he gave his name, and then they had put him into a lift and taken him, a little to his surprise, down and not up. Now he sat in a long basement-corridor watching a red light over a door; when it turned green, they had told him, he could go in, but not before. People who paid no attention to the light went in and went out; some of them carried papers and some of them brief-cases, and one was in uniform, a colonel. Nobody looked at him; he felt that he embarrassed them. They ignored him as one ignores a malformed man. But presumably it was not his limp.

Hawthorne came down the passage from the lift. He looked rumpled as though he had slept in his clothes; perhaps he had been on an all-night plane from Jamaica. He too would have ignored Wormold if Wormold had not spoken.

"Hullo, Hawthorne."

"Oh, you, Wormold."

"Did Beatrice arrive safely?"

"Yes. Naturally."

"Where is she, Hawthorne?"

"I have no idea."

"What's happening here? It looks like a court-martial."

"It *is* a court-martial," Hawthorne said frostily and went into the room with the light. The clock stood at 11:25. He had been summoned for eleven.

He wondered whether there was anything they could do to him beyond sacking him, which presumably they had already done. That was probably what they were trying to decide in there. They could hardly charge him under the Official Secrets Act. He had invented secrets, he hadn't given them away. Presumably they could make it difficult for him if he tried to find a job abroad, and jobs at home were not easy to come by at his age, but he had no intention of giving them back their money. That was for Milly; he felt now as though he had earned it in his capacity as a target for Carter's poison and Carter's bullet.

At 11:35 the Colonel came out; he looked hot and angry as he strode towards the lift. There goes a hanging judge, thought Wormold. A man in a tweed jacket emerged next. He had blue eyes very deeply sunk and he needed no uniform to mark him as a sailor. He looked at Wormold accidentally and looked quickly away again like a man of integrity. He called out "Wait for me, Colonel" and went down the passage with a very slight roll as though he were back on a bridge in rough weather. Hawthorne came next, in conversation with a very young man, and then Wormold was suddenly breathless because the light was green and Beatrice was there.

"You are to go in," she said.

"What's the verdict?"

"I can't speak to you now. Where are you staying?"

He told her.

"I'll come to you at six. If I can."

"Am I to be shot at dawn?"

"Don't worry. Go in now. He doesn't like to be kept waiting."

"What's happening to you?"

She said, "Jakarta."

"What's that?"

"The end of the world," she said. "Further than Basra. Please go in."

A man wearing a black monocle sat all by himself behind a desk. He said, "Sit down, Wormold."

"I prefer to stand."

"Oh, that's a quotation, isn't it?"

"Quotation?"

"I'm sure I remember hearing that in some play—amateur theatricals. A great many years ago, of course."

Wormold sat down. He said, "You've no right to send her to Jakarta."

"Send who to Jakarta?"

"Beatrice."

"Who's she? Oh, that secretary of yours. How I hate these Christian names. You'll have to see Miss Jenkinson about that. She's in charge of the pool, not me, thank God."

"She had nothing to do with anything."

"Anything? Listen, Wormold. We've decided to shut down your post, and the question arises—what are we to do with you?" It was coming now. Judging from the face of the Colonel who had been one of his judges, he felt that what came would not be pleasant. The Chief took

out his black monocle and Wormold was surprised by the
baby-blue eye. He said, "We thought the best thing for
you under the circumstances would be to stay at home—
on our training staff. Lecturing. How to run a station
abroad. That kind of thing." He seemed to be swallowing
something very disagreeable. He added, "Of course, as we
always do when a man retires from a post abroad, we'll
recommend you for a decoration. I think in your case
—you were not there very long—we can hardly suggest
anything higher than an O.B.E."

ii

They greeted each other formally in a wilderness of sage-
green chairs in an inexpensive hotel near Gower Street
called the Pendennis. "I don't think I can get you a
drink," he said. "It's Temperance."

"Why did you come here then?"

"I used to come with my parents when I was a boy. I
hadn't realised about the temperance. It didn't trouble me
then. Beatrice, what's happened? Are they mad?"

"They are pretty mad with both of us. They thought I
should have spotted what was going on. The Chief had
summoned quite a meeting. His liaisons were all there,
with the War Office, the Admiralty, the Air Ministry.
They had all your reports out in front of them and they
went through them one by one. Communist infiltration in
the Government—nobody minded a memo to the Foreign
Office cancelling that one. There were economic reports—
they agreed they should be disavowed too. Only the
Board of Trade would mind. Nobody got really touchy
until the Service reports came up. There was one about
disaffection in the navy and another about refuelling
bases for submarines. The Commander said, 'There must
be some truth in these.'

"I said, 'Look at the source. He doesn't exist.'

" 'We shall look such fools,' the Commander said.
'They are going to be as pleased as Punch in Naval
Intelligence.'

"But that was nothing to what they felt when the constructions were discussed."

"They'd really swallowed those drawings?"

"It was then they turned on poor Henry."

"I wish you wouldn't call him Henry."

"They said first of all that he had never reported you sold vacuum cleaners but that you were a kind of merchant-king. The Chief didn't join in *that* hunt. He looked embarrassed for some reason, and anyway Henry—I mean Hawthorne—produced the file and all the details were on it. Of course that had never gone further than Miss Jenkinson's pool. Then they said he ought to have recognised the parts of a vacuum cleaner when he saw them. So he said he had, but there was no reason why the *principle* of a vacuum cleaner might not be applied to a weapon. After that they really howled for your blood, all except the Chief. There were moments when I thought he saw the funny side. He said to them, 'What we have to do is quite simple. We have to notify the Admiralty, the War Office and the Air Ministry that all reports from Havana for the last six months are totally unreliable.' "

"But, Beatrice, they've offered me a job."

"That's easily explained. The Commander crumbled first. Perhaps at sea one learns to take a long view. He said it would ruin the Service as far as the Admiralty was concerned. In future they would rely only on Naval Intelligence. Then the Colonel said, 'If I tell the War Office, we may as well pack up.' It was quite an impasse until the Chief suggested that perhaps the simplest plan was to circulate one more report from 59200/5—that the constructions had proved a failure and had been dismantled. There remained of course you. The Chief felt you had had valuable experience which should be kept for the use of the department rather than for the popular press. Too many people had written reminiscences lately of the Secret Service. Somebody mentioned the Official Secrets Act, but the Chief thought it might not cover your case. You should have seen them when they were balked of a victim. Of course they turned on me, but I wasn't going to be cross-examined by that gang. So I spoke out."

"What on earth did you say?"

"I told them even if I'd known I wouldn't have stopped you. I said you were working for something important, not for someone's notion of a global war that may never happen. That fool dressed up as a Colonel said something about 'your country.' I said, 'What do you mean by his country? A flag someone invented two hundred years ago? The Bench of Bishops arguing about divorce and the House of Commons shouting Ya at each other across the floor? Or do you mean the T.U.C. and British Railways and the Co-op? You probably think it's your regiment if you ever stop to think, but we haven't got a regiment—he and I.' They tried to interrupt and I said, 'Oh, I forgot. There's something greater than one's country, isn't there? You taught us that with your League of Nations and your Atlantic Pact, NATO and UNO and SEATO. But they don't mean any more to most of us than all the other letters, U.S.A. and U.S.S.R. And we don't believe you any more when you say you want peace and justice and freedom. What kind of freedom? You want your careers.' I said I sympathised with the French officers in 1940 who looked after their families; they didn't anyway put their careers first. A country is more a family than a Parliamentary system."

"My God, you said all that?"

"Yes. It was quite a speech."

"Did you believe it?"

"Not all of it. They haven't left us much to believe, have they?—even disbelief. I can't believe in anything bigger than a home, or anything vaguer than a human being."

"Any human being?"

She walked quickly away without answering among the sage-green chairs and he saw that she had talked herself to the edge of tears. Ten years ago he would have followed her, but middle-age is the period of sad caution. He watched her move away across the dreary room and he thought: Darling is a manner of speech, fourteen years between us, Milly—one shouldn't do anything to shock one's child or to injure the faith one doesn't share. She had reached the door before he joined her.

He said, "I've looked up Jakarta in all the reference-books. You can't go there. It's a terrible place."

"I haven't any choice. I tried to stay in the pool."

"Did you want the pool?"

"We could have met at the Corner House sometimes and gone to a movie."

"A ghastly life—you said it."

"You would have been part of it."

"Beatrice, I'm fourteen years older than you."

"What the hell does that matter? I know what really worries you. It's not age, it's Milly."

"She has to learn her father's human too."

"She told me once it wouldn't do my loving you."

"It's got to do. I can't love you as a one-way traffic."

"It won't be easy telling her."

"It may not be very easy to stay with me after a few years."

She said, "My darling, don't worry about that any longer. You won't be left twice."

As they kissed, Milly came in carrying a large sewing basket for an old lady. She looked particularly virtuous; she had probably started a spell of doing good deeds. The old lady saw them first and clutched at Milly's arm. "Come away, dear," she said. "The idea, where anyone can see them!"

"It's all right," Milly said, "it's only my father."

The sound of her voice separated them.

The old lady said, "Is that your mother?"

"No. His secretary."

"Give me my basket," the old lady said with indignation.

"Well," Beatrice said, "That's that."

Wormold said, "I'm sorry, Milly."

"Oh," Milly said, "it's time she learnt a little about life."

"I wasn't thinking of her. I know this won't seem to you like a real marriage . . ."

"I'm glad you are being married. In Havana I thought you were just having an affair. Of course it comes to the same thing, doesn't it, as you are both married already, but somehow it will be more dignified. Father, do you know where Tattersall's is?"

"Knightsbridge, I think, but it will be closed."

"I just wanted to explore the route."

"And you don't mind, Milly?"

"Oh, pagans can do almost anything, and you are pagans. Lucky you. I'll be back for dinner."

"So you see," Beatrice said, "it was all right after all."

"Yes. I managed her rather well, don't you think? I can do some things properly. By the way, the report about the enemy agents—surely that must have pleased them."

"Not exactly. You see, darling, it took the laboratory an hour and a half floating each stamp in water to try to find your dot. I think it was on the four hundred and eighty-second stamp, and then when they tried to enlarge it—well, there wasn't anything there. You'd either over-exposed the film or used the wrong end of the microscope."

"And yet they are giving me the O.B.E.?"

"Yes."

"And a job?"

"I doubt whether you'll keep it long."

"I don't mean to. Beatrice, when did you begin to imagine that you were . . . ?"

She put her hand on his shoulder and forced him into a shuffle, among the dreary chairs. Then she began to sing, a little out of tune, as though she had been running a long way in order to catch him up.

> Sane men surround
> You, old family friends.
> They say the earth is round—
> My madness offends.
> An orange has pips, they say,
> And an apple has rind . . .

"What are we going to live on?" Wormold asked.

"You and I can find a way."

"There are three of us," Wormold said, and she real-ised the chief problem of their future—that he would never be quite mad enough.

ABOUT THE AUTHOR

Graham Greene was born in 1904 and educated at Berkhamsted School, where his father was the headmaster. On coming down from Balliol College, Oxford, where he published a book of verse, he worked for four years as a sub-editor on *The Times*. He established his reputation with his fourth novel, *Stamboul Train*, which he classed as an "entertainment" in order to distinguish it from more serious work. In 1935 he made a journey across Liberia, described in *Journey Without Maps*, and on his return was appointed film critic of the *Spectator*. In 1926 he had been received into the Roman Catholic Church and was commissioned to visit Mexico in 1938 and report on the religious persecution there. As a result he wrote *The Lawless Roads* and, later, *The Power and the Glory*.

Brighton Rock was published in 1938 and in 1940 he became literary editor of the *Spectator*. The next year he undertook work for the Foreign Office and was sent out to Sierra Leone in 1941-43. One of his major postwar novels, *The Heart of the Matter*, is set in West Africa and is considered by many to be his finest book. This was followed by *The End of the Affair*, *The Quiet American*, a story set in Vietnam, *Our Man in Havana*, and *A Burnt-Out Case*. His most recent novels are *The Comedians*, *Travels with My Aunt*, and *The Honorary Consul*. In 1967 he published a collection of short stories under the title: *May We Borrow Your Husband?* His autobiography, *A Sort of Life*, was published in 1971.

In all, Graham Greene has written some thirty novels, "entertainments," plays, children's books, travel books, and collections of essays and short stories. He was made a Companion of Honer in 1966.